FOREIGN ASSIGNMENT

In the unstable Congo region of Africa, the state of Katanga is an oasis of calm. President Tshombe and his government are united; the country's mines and industries supply the West with copper and uranium. But others, who stand to benefit if the government go under, have plans to assassinate the President. Meanwhile, Detective Simon Brand must prevent the assassination and root out the men behind the plot — and he has just seventy-two hours in which to do it . . .

SYDNEY J. BOUNDS

FOREIGN ASSIGNMENT

Complete and Unabridged

LINFORD
Leicester

First published in Great Britain

First Linford Edition
published 2012

British Library CIP Data

Bounds, Sydney J.
    Foreign assignment. - -
    (Linford mystery library)
    1. Presidents- -Congo- -Katanga- -Fiction.
    2. Assassination- -Prevention- -Fiction.
    3. Suspense fiction. 4. Large type books.
    I. Title II. Series
    823.9'14–dc23

    ISBN 978–1–4448–0968–8

Published by
F. A. Thorpe (Publishing)
Anstey, Leicestershire

Set by Words & Graphics Ltd.
Anstey, Leicestershire
Printed and bound in Great Britain by
T. J. International Ltd., Padstow, Cornwall

This book is printed on acid-free paper

1

The Assassins

The atmosphere in Elizabethville was tense. It was hostile. The very air seemed to be charged with hatred and the threat of sudden violence and murder. There was the thin smell of fear in the air, too.

Faces seen in the street, or beneath shaded awnings, or behind shuttered windows, all reflected the electric tension. White faces and black faces both.

It was in the movement of lean, hardened bodies in safari-style combat uniforms; in the hurried steps of civilians dodging from one bar to the next. It was even in the naked black feet of a Katangese policeman on point duty.

The Congo sun burned with a harsh glare over crimson and purple bougainvillea, and over pale bleached-stone arcades and glassed-in hotel verandas. It also threw a sinister black shadow across the mouth of an evil-smelling narrow alley-way between tall office blocks as a young black boy darted through. He was in a hurry. His mission was urgent.

The boy was thin, about fourteen, and dressed in khaki shorts and shirt. His hair was black and frizzy, and gleaming white teeth shone in a cheeky face. He moved swiftly, with the graceful litheness of youth — but not for long.

Deep in the dark-shadowed alleyway, men waited for him unseen. Suddenly hands lunged at him out of nowhere to grab and to grip.

Then metal blades flashed through short arcs. The boy's startled cry ended in a blubbering, animal noise as heavy machetes hacked at his face, his arms, and his stomach. The broad steel knives sliced and slashed through quivering flesh to shatter the bone beneath.

The butchery did not take long. It was all over in seconds. The boy's hacked, mangled body sprawled in a spreading pool of blood on the ground.

And the hatchetmen looked down, almost with interest, at what they had achieved: as though it were somehow surprising that a mere stripling could be changed so swiftly from an innocent youth to an ugly corpse. They stared down at the mess of bloodied, enribboned flesh, their black faces deeply absorbed in the change from life into death. It held a kind of wonder for them. So quickly . . .

Their leader looked down, too, and grunted his satisfaction. He was a big man, broad and heavy, with a squat nose and fleshy lips. His dark skin glistened with a purple sheen. He was a man-mountain dressed in a flashy style: knife-edged gaberdine trousers of blue-grey, an orange shirt with a hand-painted tie, a loose-fitting jacket padded at the shoulders and tight across massive hips, and two-tone shoes slit at the sides to give comfort to his enormous splay feet.

He was a heavy man on his feet. He nudged the lifeless, shredded corpse of the boy, and grunted again.

The white man who stood watching spoke sharply. 'That's enough, M'Polo. Go now.'

The hatchetmen faded into the shadows and vanished silently. The big man called M'Polo hesitated momentarily, then he too cat-footed down the alley, surprisingly swift and silent for so large a man.

Now, in the alley, only the European remained.

And he bent down quickly beside the body of the dead boy. His hands searched blood-soaked pockets. He found a scrap of paper and read the words hastily scribbled in pencil. A match flared in his hand, and the paper was swiftly consumed. A brief smile twisted the white man's lips.

Then he straightened up; turned. Unnoticed, he slipped out of the alleyway into the sunlight and back into the electric atmosphere of murderous violence that brooded over Elizabethville, the capital city of the newly-declared independent state of Katanga.

There were thin smears of blood on his hands, but nobody noticed.

The time was the summer of nineteen sixty-one.

* ★ * ★ *

Leisurely, the hot African sun arched across the blue bowl of the sky. It moved to throw revealing light on to the corpse in the alleyway, and on flies settling on the now glutinous blood.

Simultaneously, the sun's rays slanted through the wooden slats of a Venetian blind covering one high window of the Hotel Livingstone, to cast a diagonal pattern of light and shade over the broad lumpy figure of Clifford Wallace of the London *Morning Post*.

Wallace wore a tropical lightweight suit that contrasted oddly with an old and battered felt hat perched atop thinning dark hair. He sat at a table, long square-tipped fingers hovering uncertainly above the discoloured keys of an equally battered portable Olympia typewriter, A filter-tipped cigarette drooped from the lower lip as he sat glaring, in silence, at the almost blank sheet of paper in the machine.

Almost blank. Not quite. The few lonely words read: 'Today is quiet in

5

Elizabethville. Like yesterday, and the day before. Everyone remains calm, despite the brooding air of impending violence which hangs over the city — '

It was quiet enough, calm enough out in the street, Wallace thought. The calm before the storm. Grimacing, he pushed back his chair and paced the hot bedroom. He lit a fresh cigarette. The hot room disturbed him; it was too bright, too clean — he missed the familiar scored Fleet Street desk in the London *Morning Post* building, with its interlocking stains from innumerable teacups, the cigarette burns, the clatter of typewriters and the shrill clangour of telephones.

This room in Elizabethville was almost clinically clean, and quiet, and bright. The tabletop was pure and unsullied. The carpet threw up a riot of colour. The walls were an unadorned pastel shade calculated to soothe away worry ... yet a frown creased Wallace's rugged, suntanned face as he pushed back a shirt cuff to glance at his watch.

He was waiting for a call. An important call. And he felt growing uncertainty as

6

he waited. Maybe there was something in it after all. Maybe he was on to something big. And if so . . .

Wallace paced the room, smoking furiously, thinking hard. The sun-warmed silence held a strange scent, pleasant yet foreign. It came from exotic tropical plants in a window box beyond the slats in the Venetian blind. After all, the *Livingstone* was one of the biggest and best hotels in the city and its guests were entitled to every luxury.

The Belgian settler, Cornelius Van Cleve, had said he would know for certain within the hour, Wallace thought. He said he was expecting a messenger. Then why had there been no call from him? He had promised.

Wallace's frown deepened. Why wasn't van Cleve playing ball?

Something must have happened to the messenger Van Cleve was expecting, Wallace decided. And that meant . . .

He took a deep breath.

He would wait no longer, he thought. He had made up his mind to do what had been asked of him. His mouth was grim as he pushed through the door, out of his room.

He would do it now. He would do it at once. He would call London.

★   ★   ★

Going to Katanga hadn't been Wallace's idea in the first place, and he still wasn't sure that he liked it. But he was stuck with it, anyway.

Suspicion had coloured his face the moment Saul Jordan, editor of the London *Morning Post*, had suggested he was getting stale and needed a change of air. The suspicion had hardened into certainty when he had learnt that Will Dixon was taking over his '*Around and About*' column for a spell . . .

His mouth tightened into a bitter line at the memory. He scowled. So they thought he was getting stale . . . and that wasn't the worst part of it, not by any means.

Jordan, smooth-faced with pale-blue eyes glimmering behind gold-rimmed spectacles, had it all lined up for him.

Cliff Wallace, Special Correspondent — in the Congo.

So they wanted to get rid of him that badly, he thought bleakly. The Congo . . .

The Congo spelt violence, massacre, and bloody atrocities. Terror stalked the land as tribe warred against tribe and the *Force Publique* mutinied. White women were subjected to mass-assault, often in full view of their children, and missionaries murdered, and the situation went rapidly from bad to worse after the United Nations moved in.

The United Nations troops were perfectly capable of indulging themselves in atrocities, too, Wallace had discovered.

Amid all the confusion, only one thing seemed to be clear. Mois Tshombe was determined to keep mineral-rich Katanga independent whatever the cost. And the cost looked like being high. The rest of the Congo was swamped in chaos, and bloody chaos at that.

And Cliff Wallace was in the middle of it, not sure he wanted any part of it. Certainly, there was a good story in the Congo — but . . .

This wasn't Soho, with a reliable London bobby just round the corner ready to take over when the going got rough. This was the dark and savage heart of Africa, and a place of brooding menace. A place where you were liable to be fired on by the local gendarmerie without much of a warning, or get a bullet in the back from some trigger-happy, power-mad U.N. soldier with no warning at all.

Fine thing, Wallace thought, that he should be here, while Dixon, back in Fleet Street, ran his column for him . . .

Wallace grimaced then. He still couldn't make up his mind whether he really wanted this assignment. He'd been in Katanga a week now. Seven whole days — and it had been quiet during that time. A brooding quiet presaging trouble. Big trouble. He could feel the tension building up all around him. He had no doubt that he had a ringside seat in a hot spot — the hottest.

That was when he met Cornelius Van Cleve and the Belgian had put his proposition to him. All right, Wallace thought irritably, so he could be right. It was possible. Anything was possible in the Congo.

So now Wallace was on his way to put through a long-distance call to Simon Brand.

*   *   *

Wallace crossed the main lounge of the Hotel Livingstone on his way to the row of telephone booths in the hall. He moved over a polished parquet floor under a large, slowly-revolving fan. Red, green and amber bottles glinted in rows on shelves behind the bar counter.

Wallace smelled the air and grinned. What was it Jordan, his editor, had said? 'You need a change of air . . . ' Well, the air in the hotel bars of Elizabethville was not all that different from the air in the hotel bars of London. For which, heaven be praised . . .

Nor was the clientele.

A blonde sat alone on a high stool with her legs crossed. Wallace took a long hard look at her legs and whistled softly,

11

appreciatively under his breath. His gaze travelled upwards. Long curving legs, shapely and nyloned, disappeared discreetly beneath a short, hip-hugging skirt of bottle green. A broad silver belt encircled her waist — a belt as fascinating as its owner. An engraved belt. The chased design revealed Pan playing his flute and satyrs pursuing nymphs through a scene of bacchanalian revelry.

Wallace blinked. It was some seconds before his gaze lifted to the lime-green safari shirt that was tucked into the belt, a shirt with cleavage. He noted with approval that the blonde's breathing was deep and regular.

So absorbed was Cliff Wallace that he barked his shins on a small table as he crossed the lounge. He felt no pain. But he moved more slowly from now on, so that he could give the girl his full attention with safety.

Her face was a suntanned oval, haloed by her silver-blonde hair; there was a hint of invitation in her eyes and in her slightly parted orange-coloured lips . . .

Something about her suddenly clicked

into a slot in Wallace's mind. Now he knew who she was. Angela De Villiers of the *Johannesburg Sun* — South African correspondent. So far, he knew her only by reputation . . .

Angela De Villiers waved a cigarette in a long green holder. She indicated an empty glass on the counter at her elbow. 'You're Cliff Wallace, aren't you? How about buying me a drink?'

Wallace hesitated. He wavered, licking his lips. Remembering this blonde's reputation, and her nickname, he positively drooled. 'Angelus,' the boys called her . . . ' Angelus Bell' . . . she was on call three times a day, the boys said with a smirk, morning noon and sunset. And she was just right for Wallace's mood, that was for sure.

His progress across the lounge had slowed to a stop. The bottles behind the bar winked at him: red, amber and green. He could take his choice. His conscience struggled and finally won — duty first.

'Give me five minutes,' he said, smiling beatifically. 'Don't go away. I'll be right back, Angela.'

And he moved off quickly, with a jaunty air, anticipating a pleasure to come.

He reached the hall of the Hotel Livingstone and stepped into the first empty phone booth, sliding the door carefully shut. He picked up the handset, and when the operator answered he said: 'I want you . . . I mean, I want London!'

2

Foreign Assignment

A dismal grey gloom hung over London's Berkeley Square, hiding the plane trees and darkening the office windows. The summer sky was the colour of slate. A damp chill seemed to seep in from outside through invisible cracks and pervade the entire building which housed Simon Brand Investigations.

It was an unusually slack period for this organisation, and the staff were gathered in the big outer office. No one had suggested this. It had just happened — as if each felt a need for mutual support from the gloomy weather and their own inactivity.

Nick Chandler had been the first to desert his post. Nick hoped that a chat with Marilyn Lane might lift his feeling of gloom. It didn't. Brand's dark-haired and pretty young receptionist sat glum-faced at her desk, doodling with a ballpoint pen; routine work had lost its savour on this cheerless day. She and Nick exchanged wan smiles. Miss Chrisp sat with the firm's account books open before her, and her mind wandering. It was that sort of day. Nobody — but nobody — felt like buckling to!

Marla Dean, Brand's slim blonde secretary, was the next to drift in, her expression downcast. She said: 'Let's make a pot of tea, Marilyn. It might help to cheer us all up.'

Even Molly, the seal-point Siamese cat, stepping daintily behind Marla, seemed to have lost some of her aloofness and appeared almost glad to share the others' company. But she would have preferred sherry . . .

Marilyn Lane rose quickly. It was something — anything — to do. Nick picked up a copy of the *Morning Post* and turned the pages listlessly. Marla stared through the windows at the grey gloom outside.

Then Brand stepped from his private office. He stopped in the doorway to light

16

a cigarette, regarding them thoughtfully with blue-grey eyes. His mobile lips moved in sympathy. He, too, felt oppressed. And it wasn't only due to the weather, he thought. They'd all been going flat-out just lately. Now, due to a brisk winding-up of a difficult case, reaction had set in. They hadn't got back to routine yet. This must rate as the quietest day of the year.

Marla turned with a sigh. 'Oh, for a trip abroad — couldn't we be offered a case somewhere the sun is shining?'

Nick looked up from the *Morning Post*. 'Like Cliff?' he suggested. 'He's in a hotspot all right. It says here — '

'Oh, no — not the Congo,' Marla said quickly. 'Anywhere but there.'

That was when the phone rang and Marilyn jumped, nearly scalding herself as she filled the teapot. Marla crossed quickly to the switchboard. 'I'll take it,' she said briskly. The rest looked at Marla intently, alert now.

She lifted the receiver, and listened. Then she said, startled: 'Talk of the devil!'

She looked at Brand.

'It's Cliff Wallace,' she said. 'And he

wants you! He's calling from the Congo!'

Brand took the call. As he cupped the telephone to his ear, he heard Cliff Wallace's voice, faint with long-distance travelling:

'Hello! Brand? Listen — ! I'm on to something that I think will interest you. Something red hot. Someone I've met here in Elizabethville needs your help badly. A Belgian. He asked me to contact you. He wants you to fly out here right away. He's offering you all expenses and ten thousand pounds plus . . . to prevent a murder!'

One of Brand's black eyebrows jerked upwards. 'Whose murder is that?'

Wallace was cagey. 'That would be telling.'

Brand said thoughtfully: 'Ten thousand pounds . . . ? It's a lot of money — '

'Too right it is,' Wallace cut in. 'But it's all yours if you want it. And, believe me, the job you have to do to earn it has certain intriguing qualities, and it's right up your street. So what do you say?'

'For a start,' Brand told his friend, 'I'm afraid I'm going to repeat what I said a minute ago. Just tell me — whose murder?'

But there was no answer from Wallace.

'Look,' Brand said. 'You know me, Cliff. And you know that once I commit myself and say that I'll take on a job, I'm really committed, body and soul. That's the way I'm made. But — ' his voice hardened, ' — I'm not in the habit of just jumping off in the dark. I need to know more than you've told me before I agree to fly half way round the world. So suppose you start answering my questions. What's this all about? Fill me in.'

But Wallace sounded firm, though regretful. 'No can do, Brand. I'm sorry . . .'

He added: 'I'd hesitate to give you details over any telephone line, and on this particular one it's absolutely out of the question. Who knows who's listening? And this is big stuff! Believe me, Brand, one hell of a lot could hang on whether you'll come out here or not. Say you will. Your tickets will be waiting for you at the London office of Sabena. You'll get top priority — VIP treatment. For you're needed out here, and needed desperately, and for once in my life I'm not exaggerating. Honest men are in short supply in this part of the Congo right now.'

'But you've got the United Nations there,' Brand pointed out, and Wallace's reply was short and succinct. Then — 'Brand — you will come? You've got to!'

'I don't know . . . ' Still the detective was rather uncertain. 'Before I commit myself I'd like to know more.'

'Hell!' At the other end of the line, Wallace swore explosively. Then he said: 'All right, Brand. All right. I can just tell you this much more as a clincher. Now, listen carefully . . . ' And his voice dropped into a significant and confidential key.

★　★　★

An hour and a half later, two lightweight suitcases stood packed, ready and waiting in Simon Brand's Berkeley Square office, and Brand himself was making a last-minute phone call to check final details of his forthcoming flight.

He had made up his mind. He was going to the Congo in answer to Cliff Wallace's call. And he was taking Nick Chandler, his young partner, with him.

Marla Dean's dark blue eyes misted over as she watched Brand at the phone. Tall and erect behind his desk, he looked leaner and more attractive than ever, she thought, in that crisp linen suit with the broad slash of brown tie against a soft cream-coloured shirt. He looked very masculine, tough, and efficient, and it was stupid to worry, she told herself. But still a shadow of doubt darkened her mind. Would he come through the Congo upheaval unscathed?

Nick Chandler also stood close at hand, eyeing his chief as he spoke into the phone. And Marla couldn't help noticing that Nick's expression betrayed an inner, bubbling excitement. He would feel the call to the Congo as a call to action, she thought. And action was something that Nick could not have enough of.

Waiting for Brand to finish his phone

call, Nick shifted a manilla folder from one hand to the other.

The folder contained clippings from the world's press, detailing the troubled history of the Congo. It was a file Brand proposed to study on the flight out.

But Marla had already scanned through all the clippings. It was she who had assembled the file. And this was the chief reason she found it hard not to worry about what fate might have in store for Brand and for Nick when they reached the Congo. The contents of the manilla folder that Nick was holding made very grim reading indeed . . . Assailed from all sides by international pressure groups which mouthed lofty sentiments but which were all greedy for personal gain of one kind or another, Belgium had been coerced into granting her territory of the Congo full independence too swiftly, too soon. This had been recognised by everybody — only when it was too late!

The result could hardly have failed to please the hard-faced men in the Kremlin whose fellow-travellers the world over had vied with the faceless men of Wall Street and the United States copper trusts to make the position of the Belgians in the Congo truly untenable. For that result was disaster.

The Congolese *Force Publique*, the armed organisation charged with the task of impartially maintaining law and order throughout the country after the Belgians' abdication of their authority, straightway became a pawn in an undercover political war. Free elections, conducted before the Belgians had left, had brought a shaky coalition government to office in Leopoldville, and a thin, gangling politico by the name of Patrice Lumumba to the position of premier. But, with this situation, Lumumba himself was far from being satisfied. His ambition wasn't realised.

But let him only demonstrate to the other members of the coalition government that he had the rank and file of the armed *Force Publique* behind him, he thought, and none would dare to oppose his ambition.

This was his plan. But something went wrong.

Lumumba certainly whipped up the native Congolese troops to a frenzy without any difficulty. But then he couldn't control them. He had incited them to turn on their European officers, for the brutal beatings of a score or so Belgians would be as good a demonstration of his power over the soldiery as anything else, and it would also serve as an object lesson to his colleagues in government. The unstated threat was; first white men — then black, if they would not toe the line. But, once started, the violence did not end there.

After turning on their Belgian officers, the *Force Publique* went berserk. A wave of rapine, pillage and murder swept over the country like a great forest fire.

Everywhere, Europeans were arrested and beaten, many of the men slaughtered and the women debauched. They were held captive together, locked-up and tied-up in looted, half-ruined houses like beasts in their stalls to satisfy their captors.

As the atrocities mounted in intensity, the few Europeans who remained alive and at liberty fled hurriedly. Then, as if this was some long awaited signal, the last vestige of the coalition government's authority collapsed in the dust, and tribal warfare broke out. And this was only the beginning.

Alarmed at what was happening in the rest of the Congo, and fearful that chaos and murder might soon invade the so-far peaceful province of Katanga, in July 1960, Moise Tshombe declared the province an independent republic, and seceded from union with the rest of the country. Now the situation deteriorated even more rapidly.

By the early months of 1961, the Congo had split into fiercely warring factions. All the time, fighting raged — grim, savage fighting. And terror spread, rapine, savage murder, and barbaric torture.

Now the provinces of Leopoldville and Equator were tenuously held by a Central Congolese government led by President Kasavubu and recognised by the United Nations. Orientale, in the north, was controlled by the Communist puppet,

25

Antoine Gizenga, with his headquarters in Stanleyville, and it was here Patrice Lumumba fled into hiding after he had been rudely ousted from his post as Prime Minister. The fickle rank and file of the *Force Publique* had found other demagogues to listen to now. Elsewhere in the country, Kasai province was split into two rival groups, whilst Kivu had no effective administration at all. And, in the south-east, Tshombe held on to Katanga, helped by native Katangese and European residents alike, all hoping to keep some vestige of civilization alive in this progressive and rich industrial heart of the Congo . . .

This, therefore, was the situation into which Brand and Nick would soon be winging their way, in an urgent attempt to prevent an assassination in a land torn by modern greed and primitive vengeance. A country of chaos. They would be flying out of the dull grey gloom over London to meet savage violence in the baking and blistering sun.

Brand finished his telephone call, and straightened up. He smiled, and said briefly to Marla, and Lorna Chrisp, and Marilyn Lane: 'See you all soon . . . come on, Nick.'

Nick Chandler picked up his grip with a nonchalant air. 'So long, Marilyn . . . '

'Good luck,' chorused Marilyn, Lorna Chrisp and Marla.

In the doorway, Brand paused and turned. Poker-faced, he said: 'I don't expect we'll be gone all that long. In the meantime, hold the fort and mind you don't get up to mischief . . . '

He went out. Nick followed him, Congo bound.

Molly, the seal-point Siamese, arched her back and rubbed her soft fur against Marla Dean's nyloned legs. And she purred. Four females together . . . with the boss away. She hoped they wouldn't take too much notice of Brand's injunction not to get up to mischief . . .

With any luck, it wouldn't be long before they got out the sherry.

3

The Belgian

Cliff Wallace was right in at least one respect. Brand and Chandler were treated as V.I.Ps. They were given every facility and assistance. Their passage was smoothed from the moment they drove into London Airport.

A great silver bird awaited them, one of the newest aircraft of the Sabena fleet. It was fast and luxurious, and the hostess as attractive as she was efficient. She provided drinks and cigarettes, and tempted them with delicacies that would have delighted a gourmet. The other passengers on the flight included several hard-faced young men who looked tough and adventurous enough to be on their way to join Tshombe's Katanga army.

Brand and Nick settled back in deep and comfortable seats to read and digest the file of cuttings that Marla had compiled at such short notice. They studied the clippings assiduously, comparing notes, and absorbing the political background to the disastrous events in the Congo. They were eager to learn all they could from the multifarious reports that had appeared in the world's press. Both had a feeling that they could not be too well prepared for the task that lay ahead of them.

They flew south, like migratory birds, across the Mediterranean, over North Africa, across the Sahara. The plane touched down at Kano, in Nigeria, and they stretched their legs whilst it was refuelled. Then they took off again for the dark equatorial heart of Africa, the Congo river, and the rain-belt forests — the country of Stanley and Livingstone. The sun's brilliant rays shafted down, dappling the vivid green of the treetops.

'It looks peaceful enough,' Nick ventured, staring down through the cabin window, watching the plane's shadow across the rolling grassy hills of the savanna.

Brand smiled grimly. 'A bird's-eye view

of any country can be deceptive,' he said.

On the ground, he guessed, it would be hot, fly-ridden, and dangerous. Very dangerous. Violence would lurk in the brush, in the shadows, everywhere. There would be men in hiding, men in uniforms with guns, badly frightened and desperate men, vengeful and self-seeking men. Black men and white.

Now they passed over Katanga province on the final lap of their journey. Below them, a semi-barren desolate land was scarred with opencast mines and quarries, and the tall smokestacks of a smelting plant.

'Fasten your seatbelts, please,' the pretty Belgian airhostess said. 'We are about to land . . . '

* * *

Viewed from the air, as the Sabena airliner lost height, the city of Elizabethville, the capital of the newly-declared state of Katanga, was seen as a formal pattern of wide tree-shaded avenues and plazas in the American style. The industrial, residential and business sections were all separately zoned. There was nothing crude or rough and ready about the layout of this typically modern cathedral city. Both Brand and Tinker were very impressed.

Just outside the town was the palace, President Tshombe's palace. A red brick and concrete mansion, a juxtaposition of the European and the African. It was walled, showy, dramatic.

'Like Hampton Court Palace — with knobs on,' Nick commented.

As the plane circled, Brand was staring with compressed lips at the army encampment opposite the palace. The headquarters of the United Nations forces in Katanga; was the encampment placed where it was purely by chance?

Brand hardly thought so. He thought it would have been sited opposite the palace as a deliberately provocative gesture: a slap in the face for President Tshombe, who deeply resented the presence of alien and hostile troops in his country.

All this boded ill for any peaceful settlement of the differences between

Katanga and the United Nations, Simon Brand thought.

And then the silver bird of Sabena touched down on the main runway of Elizabethville Airport.

*   *   *

The snarling roar of the aero-engines died. A hatch opened, and wheeled steps were rolled into position. Brand ducked through the opening and went down the steps — to come face to face with armed men, grimly waiting.

He saw the glint of sunlight on naked steel bayonets; saw itching fingers curled about the triggers of deadly sub-machineguns. Hard, bleak eyes stared back at him.

The armed men were soldiers wearing blue steel helmets and United Nations armbands. The world's peacemakers. Simon Brand's mouth moved rather wryly. He had known friendlier welcomes than this in his time.

Then the clipped, coldly-polite voice of the U.N. Guard commander challenged him, demanding his name, his passport, his business, and Simon Brand frowned. The thought occurred to him that the troops of the United Nations were wrongly interpreting their role here as that of an army of occupation. This was precisely how they were acting, and Brand didn't like it. He answered the guard commander quietly, but very offhandedly, and looked around thoughtfully as he did so, sampling the atmosphere of Elizabethville.

There was tension in the air. The atmosphere was one of the grimmest foreboding. Violence was threatening. Brand could feel it. Then, some distance away, he saw a group of Katangese gendarmes. They were watching the U.N. men. They were eyeing them narrowly. Their gaze was sharp, missing nothing. And Brand sensed bitter hostility between the two groups of men — something that did not augur well for the future.

He turned his attention on the U.N. guard commander again.

More questions were asked. Brand answered them. He stood with Nick and waited with as much patience as he could muster for the formalities to end. Overhead, the sky was a vast bowl of blue and the sun a disc of burnished copper. But a cool breeze sighed gently over the field. The air sparkled. Though they were only twelve degrees south of the equator, Brand thought, they were four thousand feet above sea level and that fact made quite a difference.

The U.N. guard commander asked his last question of Brand, was answered, and handed back the detective's passport. The officer then began a coldly polite interrogation of Nick while Brand moved his feet a little impatiently and listened to a babel of tongues in the background: French, Flemish, Ethiopian, Congolese, Hindi, Swedish —

A familiar English voice suddenly cut across all the others. 'Brand! There you are! At last . . . '

'Cliff! It's good to see at least one friendly, smiling face.'

The detective and the *Morning Post's* special correspondent grinned at each other as they shook hands. Cliff Wallace looked almost pale beside the deeply tanned faces all around. 'This is the first time you've been outside the hotel's bar, I'll bet,' Simon Brand smiled.

Wallace reached for Brand's suitcase. 'This way,' he said forcefully, brandishing an impressive-looking pass at the U.N. security men. 'You're wasting your time,' he told the guard commander. 'These gentlemen are two V.I.Ps. Very important indeed. I'll vouch for them personally.'

And not brooking any interference or argument, he led Brand and Nick briskly across the tarmac.

He whisked them past sentries and out through the main gate. A car waited in the roadway beyond with a beautiful girl behind the wheel. The car was a bright, shiny-new emerald green Studebaker, and the girl was equally dazzling.

She was a provocatively curved silver-blonde with a short, ultra-tight skirt and a safari shirt. Encircling a miniscule waist beneath bold, jutting breasts was a broad, engraved silver belt.

Brand's gaze travelled from the engraved silver belt to the girl's face, and then he noticed that Nick's eyes hadn't travelled at all. They were still riveted on the belt. It was a good gimmick, the detective decided. It captured interest — while its owner had those extra few seconds to size up the opposition.

Wallace swung the lightweight suitcases into the back of the car. 'Angela De Villiers,' he said in introduction. 'She works for the *Johannesburg Sun*. Angela — meet Simon Brand and Nick Chandler.'

'I've heard of you, of course,' Angela De Villiers told Simon Brand coolly, her gaze raking his face with intense, searching scrutiny. There could be no doubt about it, Brand thought: the South African girl was curious about the reason for his arrival here in Katanga.

Meanwhile, Nick was murmuring confidentially into Wallace's ear. 'You seem to be doing well for yourself here, Cliff, you old reprobate you!'

Wallace smiled, and climbed in beside the blonde while Nick joined Brand in the back of the car. 'The Livingstone, Angy,' Wallace told the girl. 'And make it snappy. We've got some important business to attend to. Very important.' He grinned. 'Unfinished business!'

The Studebaker leapt forward, quickly gathering speed. The South African girl handled the car like a racing driver. And as it roared off down the road Brand saw a mob converge on the airport.

It was an angry mob, shouting abuse. He saw glistening black faces and hands gripping clubs, knives, and stakes. It looked like trouble was about to break. The roar of the crowd rose in volume.

Wallace twisted round in his seat. 'It looks like the U.N. have just taken over the airfield and sealed it off. I heard that was about to happen. The local people won't like it. They won't like it at all.'

He shook his head.

He said: 'I'm glad I'm not wearing a U.N. armband. Believe me, the United Nations haven't made themselves very popular here.'

The car passed swiftly along a wide, tree-shaded road to enter Elizabethville. Brand saw glassed-in terraces and white stone arcades — and an anthill, the size of a two-storey house, between tall office blocks. Outside a cinema a U.N. car stood abandoned, its tyres slashed to ribbons.

Faces on the sidewalk — white faces and black faces — were tense and expectant.

Angela De Villiers said flatly: 'Not just a holiday trip, I think, Mr. Brand?'

'Not just a holiday trip,' Brand agreed but said nothing more.

The Studebaker swung through the Place de l'Etoile and braked to a halt in front of the Hotel Livingstone. Then Brand heard it — distinctly.

From the direction of the airfield they had just left came the first ripples of gunfire.

$\star$ $\star$ $\star$

Fifteen minutes later, after a quick shower, Brand and Nick descended the broad main staircase of the Hotel Livingstone and walked into the lounge.

Wallace and Angela De Villiers were at the bar, talking with a squat, powerfully built man dressed in a grey lightweight suit. Wallace waved as they crossed the polished parquet floor.

He said: 'You'll try a local brew? I can recommend it.' When Brand and Nick nodded, Wallace turned to the barman. 'Two Simbas . . . '

The black-skinned bartender skimmed the foam from the glasses with a piece of carved ivory before pushing them across the counter. Brand sipped experimentally. It was a cool, refreshing, full-bodied drink: like the best Belgian beer.

'Good,' he said finally. 'Very good.' And Nick nodded agreement.

'You are surprised, Mr. Brand?' Wallace's companion, the man in the grey lightweight suit, spoke good English with a Flemish accent. 'You need not be. Simba is the best beer brewed in Africa today.'

'That I can believe,' Brand said smiling.

Wallace interposed quickly, speaking to Brand. 'This is Mr. Cornelius Van Cleve. The man you'll want to talk to.'

Brand appraised Van Cleve very carefully. Dark lensed glasses rested on a prominent nose. The eyes behind the lenses were hooded and hidden. Massive tortoiseshell earpieces disappeared into a mass of very dark, shaggy hair in which there was no hint of grey, even though Brand judged the man's age to be around fifty.

Brand thought that Van Cleve was a man who knew how to look after himself physically, nor was this the only conclusion he came to. There was a quality of rock-like hardness in the man; an air of cold-blooded, ruthless calculation. Cornelius Van Cleve, he thought, was a man who could be very tough indeed.

'We shall have dinner together, Mr. Brand,' Van Cleve now said quietly. 'I have already booked a table — for three.'

As he spoke, he stared directly — and pointedly — at Wallace and the blonde Angela.

The journalist's craggy face split in a lopsided grin. 'Don't tell me,' he said wryly. 'Just let me guess ... I'm not wanted around here.' And he winked at Angela. 'Well, sweetheart,' he drawled, 'luckily we've still got each other ... '

As they moved off, the blonde clutched Wallace's arm in a tight, proprietary hold. She became a clinging vine. Brand wondered about her — and reserved judgment.

Not so Van Cleve. Under the gently swishing fan, a tanned hand gestured restlessly. A hand with strong fingers. 'That South African girl,' he growled. 'I don't trust her. She wants to know too much.'

Then he led the way across the floor.

Brand and Nick followed across the lounge and into the dining room. There were great palms set in tubs, a haze of cigarette smoke, a babble of conversation. Waiters glided silently between the tables where sat the local élite, white and black, formally suited, their ladies fashionably gowned. Yet there was an air of tension here too, Brand noted, as Van Cleve led them to a reserved table in a secluded corner.

Just as they reached their table, a man suddenly stepped around one of the screening palms. 'Hello there, Van Cleve,' he said smoothly. 'It's nice to see fresh faces in E'ville — won't you introduce me to your two friends?'

He extended a soft white hand that the

Belgian pointedly ignored.

But he answered the man, clearly because he could think of no other way to get rid of him quickly. Lips curled in distaste, he grunted an introduction: 'Declan O'Donovan — with the U.N. delegation here. Mr. Brand and Mr. Chandler — '

Declan O'Donovan was a beanpole of man with sandy hair and watery eyes. He moved with a certain fluid grace, a sinuosity that brought a swift unspoken response to Brand's mind. 'Spineless,' he thought — and then corrected himself. 'Not spineless. Boneless.'

'Mr. Brand, you said — ?' O'Donovan was echoing the name, thin head cocked to one side calculatingly. 'Well, well, that is interesting. Very interesting indeed.'

His smile was sickly, his voice high and shrill. 'I'm with the United Nations political delegation. No connection with the armed forces, of course. None whatsoever, Frankly, I deplore this invasion — ' he used the word delicately ' — this invasion by the great powers. It may well upset domestic harmony.'

He glanced at their table set with three places.

'I wonder, now,' he said, 'if you would mind if I joined you . . . ?'

Van Cleve glared at him. This was plainly too much. He said curtly: 'Sorry, O'Donovan. We have private business to discuss.'

'Ah . . . private business, is it?' O'Donovan's shrill voice softened a fraction. His gaze moved from face to face, probing and curious. He sighed: 'Well, then, I'll run along. Hope to meet you again, Mr. Brand — before you have to leave us.'

There was something almost ominous in that last turn of phrase. But Brand replied levelly: 'I expect we shall bump into each other again, Mr. O'Donovan.'

The United Nations man regarded him thoughtfully for a moment before turning away. He then walked straight out of the dining room. It seemed that he was no longer hungry.

Van Cleve dropped heavily into a chair, scowling as he did so. 'Damned U.N. snooper!' he growled. 'Poking his nose into everyone's business! They're just like buzzards, some of the United Nations' types that have descended upon us. They're waiting for Katanga to die — wanting the country to die! They're just like buzzards, hoping to rip the entrails out of this state while they're still warm!' He almost spat. Then he leaned forward. 'Let me order our meal, gentlemen,' he said, 'and then dismiss the waiter quickly. Here, in this corner, we cannot be overheard once the waiter has left us, and we have a great deal to talk about and all of it is of vital importance.'

His voice dropped to a significant level.

'What we talk about here tonight may well determine whether a certain very important man lives or dies. Whether he's murdered . . . or whether you save him,' he said.

4

Power Politics

Declan O'Donovan walked from the Hotel Livingstone's dining room. Once round the corner, out of sight, his pace quickened. His expression was worried. He'd tried to gatecrash Van Cleve's little party and had been given the brush-off . . . but he still had to know what Brand was up to. It was imperative that he found out.

Brand's sudden appearance in Elizabethville had set him wondering. The detective might upset his plans. If only Van Cleve hadn't been so suspicious he might have learnt something. As it was . . .

O'Donovan smiled then: a sudden, cunning smile. There were other ways of getting the information he needed. Oh, yes . . . yes, indeed!

Without doubt there were most certainly other ways of getting at Simon Brand!

Cornelius Van Cleve sat with his broad back against one wall of the Hotel Livingstone's dining room.

He removed his dark glasses and polished the lenses with a silk handkerchief. He replaced the glasses carefully on his large beak of a nose, and peered intently all round the room.

There were no waiters within earshot.

Only when Van Cleve had assured himself of this fact did he lean forward and speak in a low tone that carried as far as the ears of Simon Brand and Nick Chandler — and no farther. Nevertheless, he spoke forcefully.

They had nearly finished their meal: an excellent one, considering that elsewhere in the Congo Red Cross planes were rushing emergency airdrops of relief food parcels to famine areas. In Elizabethville, in the Hotel Livingstone, they had dined richly on shrimps and asparagus, creamed chicken in mushroom sauce, and rich cakes filled with mousse. Now, over coffee and cigarettes, Brand and Nick settled back in comfort to listen to the broad, burly Belgian.

Van Cleve said, 'The situation in Katanga, gentlemen, is — so far — distinct from the one ruling the rest of the Congo. Katanga is an oasis amid chaos. The government of President Tshombe is united, and the administration still works. Belgian technicians have returned from Rhodesia to help. With the mines and industries, it is business as usual — so far. Order prevails. And it must remain that way.

'Now — ' the Belgian went on, 'this state of affairs depends very largely upon one mortal man — President Moise Tshombe. And do not I beg of you make the mistake of thinking him a mere puppet dangling from Belgian strings. Nothing could be further from the real truth. It is a fact that sometimes our interests and his coincide, but more often than not he uses us for his own purposes.'

'Us . . . ?' Brand probed gently.

Van Cleve gestured. 'We'll come to that in a moment. Just let us get this established once and for all. Moise

47

Tsbombe is the strong man of Katangese politics, and be may yet prove to be the saviour of the whole Congo. Mark my words well. And something else is quite certain. He will never fall for the communist line.'

Brand murmured quietly, 'I'll accept all you've said. But now let's return to my question. You — Mr. Van Cleve. You, I take it, represent the Union Miniere? It was this company you were talking about when you used the word 'us'?'

Van Cleve hesitated fractionally, then he nodded. 'Yes,' he said. 'I do represent the Union Miniere du Haut Katanga. The approach I made to you through Mr. Wallace has the company's complete approval . . . and backing. But before we go any further let me clear away any false misconceptions that you may have about the company I represent. It seems to be generally believed the Union Miniere is exclusively Belgian, and concerned only with the exploitation of this part of the Congo — giving nothing at all in return. Both conceptions are completely false.

'To begin with, the company's stock is

48

internationally owned. Your own London-dominated Tanganyika Concessions holds a large block of the shares, and the democratically elected government of Katanga itself holds another. My own country's holding is vested in the Société Generale, with its headquarters in Brussels, and *its* stockholders are legion. Not only is the Union Miniere an exclusively Belgian concern, it is not controlled by a tight-knit ring of international financiers either. Let us lay that ghost once and for all. And as for the other canard —

'It is said that the Union Miniere exploits and depresses the poor down-trodden Katangese native. Gentlemen, whoever says this has obviously never come here to Katanga. You have, and you can see for yourself how much truth there is in this — this Communist propaganda.

'The Union Miniere houses its workers — and not in slums, but in well-planned townships. It educates them. It provides them with doctors. It has built and staffed hospitals. It provides transport services, and every modern facility to its employ-ees. And all this is in addition to the millions it pours, month by month, into the public coffers of this state of Katanga, in dividends and in taxation. Gentlemen, every thirty days, funds in excess of three and a half million United States dollars flow from my company into the treasury of this state of Katanga. Do you wonder that you'll never hear a Katangese criticise the Union Miniere?'

Simon Brand shook his bead. He already knew quite a lot about the Union Miniere, and about the Société Generale too. This last company had enormous industrial ramifications.

Through the Union Miniere, it dealt in copper, cobalt, silver, platinum, tungsten; the Katanga copper deposits were the richest in the world; it supplied eighty percent of the world's cobalt. It was a gigantic combine with numerous outlets; Sogelec for distributing hydro-electrical power; Sogechim, the chemical branch of the colossus; it held a large shareholding in Sabena airlines.

The industrial empire of the Société Generale had its roots deep not only in Katanga but throughout all of the Congo.

It was part of the social fabric of the country.

Simon Brand knew all this —

Cornelius Van Cleve said casually, 'But perhaps you didn't know that the Katanga uranium deposits are significant, too? Uranium from Shinkolobwe mine, ninety miles north of E'ville, was shipped direct to the United States for the 'Manhattan project'. Do you understand me? Edgar Sengier, head of Union Minire, arranged that during the early part of the last war. It was uranium from this part of the Congo that made possible the atom bombs dropped on Hiroshima and Nagasaki . . . '

He paused, and his voice hardened.

'Without Union Miniere, no atomic bombs could have been made at all. I suggest that this has its importance, too.'

Simon Brand nodded. He had heard a rumour about the Sengier story. He was impressed to have confirmation on the spot.

All this,' Van Cleve went on, 'is vital to the West. You can see that? I fear that the Americans can't. You know why? Because they don't know the truth, the whole truth, the facts. These are kept from them by powerful and greedy men who are not concerned about making the world safe for democracy. They are only concerned about making money. So they play the Communists' game. Support for the disruptive United Nations' intervention in Katanga is coming from the powerful United States copper lobby. These gentlemen would like to see the Union Miniere put out of business, and world copper prices rocket and soar. Theirs is a selfish and short-term view. Their objective — lining their pockets. My view, and the view of my company is a different thing altogether.

'We seek to preserve the Union Miniere — not only as a profit-making industrial concern, but also as a powerful weapon in the armoury of the West. We cannot and will not just walk out of Katanga. There is too much at stake. And President Tshombe is the one man who can keep Katanga going . . . '

Nick stubbed out the butt of his cigarette. He stubbed it out in a gleaming glass ashtray reposing in the centre of a dazzling white tablecloth. He said, 'But for how long? When we came from the airport, there was a mob going into action. We heard shooting.'

Van Cleve inclined his head. 'It is true, Mr. Chandler. There have been riots; some minor disorders. All true and no one pretends to be happy about it. This has been caused by the flagrant provocation offered by the troops of the United Nations.

'But — ' he went on, and he gestured with a strong, thick-fingered hand, 'these civil disorders must never be allowed to engulf Katanga in the chaos that has swallowed up the other parts of the Congo . . . '

He gestured again.

'President Tshombe is the keystone,' he said. And his piercing gaze stabbed at Brand and at Tinker. 'And now we come to the reason that I asked you to fly out here to Elizabethville . . . '

His voice hardened.

'Suppose Moise Tshombe were killed. Suppose he were to be murdered . . . *what then?*'

5

Deadline for Murder

Silence followed Van Cleve's words: *what then?*

A taut silence.

Slowly, Brand grew aware of the background hum of conversation; the muted tinkling of cutlery through the dining room. He asked quietly: 'What do you want us to do?'

Van Cleve did not answer directly. Instead, he repeated: 'Suppose Tshombe were killed ... Katanga would fall apart overnight. Chaos would follow inevitably. The Lumumbist forces in the north have Communist backing — I don't need to tell you that, Mr. Brand. Even now they are gathering just over the border, in Kivu. They would sweep southwards together with their allies, the Baluba ... and do you really believe that the United Nations could

54

— or would — hold them back?'

Bitterness crept into the Belgian's guttural voice.

'The calibre of the United Nations' troops is not of the best. U.N. propagandists describe Katanga's white officers and soldiers as 'mercenaries' and the Communist press the world over gleefully echoes the phrase. The Communists love the picture that it evokes — an army of hired white killers, remnants of colonialism at its worst. Nothing could be further from the truth!

'Agreed, Katanga has accepted the services of a few foreign-born trained soldiers. But what underdeveloped country does not need foreign assistance? The United States sends thousands of officers and men abroad every year, and spends millions of dollars on its military aid programmes. Besides, in Katanga's case, the foreign-born men attached to its army are very few in number indeed.

'Most of the so-called 'mercenaries' are, in fact, Katanga-born and Katanga-bred — even if they are of European stock. They have their roots here: their homes and their families. These men are Africans, gentlemen, and it doesn't matter whether their skins are black, white, or khaki. They are Africans in the fullest and broadest sense of the word, and why should they be denied the right to fight for everything that they hold dear?

'Why should they be expected to stand idly by and see the terror mount all around them and not lift a finger to check it? Is it reasonable that they should see murder, and worse than murder, threaten their wives and their children and not be allowed to protect them?'

Van Cleve's voice dripped sudden scorn. 'I ask you . . . these men are 'mercenaries', gentlemen . . . ?'

He didn't wait for the only — the obvious — answer.

'No,' he said heavily. 'The United Nations' troops are the real mercenaries here. Every man jack of them is fighting for money in a conflict in which he has no other stake than his pay. And, like many true mercenaries, the troops of the United Nations have little stomach for a real fight. Which brings us back to what I said earlier. I doubt if the U.N. could stop Lumumbist forces invading Katanga if Tshombe were to be killed.

'Far too many of the mercenaries employed by the United Nations are little better than thugs. They are sweepings of the prisons of Addis Ababa and points north. They're better at bullying civilians here in Elizabethville than they are at fighting. Make no mistake about this. With President Tshombe dead, Katanga would be given over to the same monstrous, murderous terror that has already engulfed the rest of the Congo!'

There, briefly, he paused.

Then, very gravely, he said: 'The danger of this happening is very close; Very real. We would not have been so desperately anxious to have you come out here at such short notice were this not so.'

He said: 'The fact is, gentlemen — ' and his voice hardened ' — we have discovered that there is a plot afoot at this moment to kill President Tshombe, and to kill him very soon.'

His face was grim.

He said: 'Unless you can do something

to stop it, President Tshombe is going to be murdered in the next seventy-two hours!'

A frown creased Simon Brand's forehead. His eyes were intent upon Cornelius van Cleve. He said: 'But if you know this much and you're certain of it, I don't quite see — '

'I know of the existence of the plot, Mr. Brand. But that's all I do know. I have no inkling of the identity of the would-be assassins.'

Nick drew a deep breath. He said: 'So we're to be elected as President Tshombe's bodyguard. Is that the idea?'

The Belgian shook his head, 'No. Not at all. Moise Tshombe already has a bodyguard . . . naturally. No, what I want you to do is just this — first, prevent the assassination attempt and second, expose the man behind it. This man must be someone close to Tshombe. Only in that way could he hope to succeed. Someone trusted — ' bitterness edged his voice ' — a personal friend.'

A cold light flickered in the Belgian's hard-muscled face.

'The guilty man must be someone apparently above suspicion. Unfortunately, that doesn't narrow the circle of suspects very much. President Tshombe moves among a large crowd of followers: Belgians, European advisers, his own people. The man we're looking for could be any one of these — '

Brand interrupted. 'All right — suppose we identify this man for you. What then?'

Van Cleve's voice was harsh. 'You may safely leave that part of it in my hands, Mr. Brand. Once you have identified the man, I shall know what to do. The administration of justice in the Congo today devolves upon the strongest; it is the law of the jungle all over again. You need have no fear that the guilty will go unpunished.'

He looked directly at Simon Brand and his gaze was challenging. 'Well — what do you say? I am authorised to offer you ten thousand pounds and all your incidental expenses if you will take on the job of frustrating this premeditated act of murder and expose the man responsible.

Well, Mr. Brand — Mr. Chandler — will you do it?'

Simon Brand stirred in his chair. He blew a thin plume of cigarette smoke and thoughtfully watched it disperse in the air-stream of an electric fan.

Nick was eyeing him keenly. So was Cornelius Van Cleve. Silence reigned for a very long moment. Then — 'All right,' Brand said. 'All right, we'll take the job on.' And he looked from the burly Belgian to Nick and back again. 'But it isn't going to be easy,' he said.

Cornelius Van Cleve could not agree more.

'It certainly isn't going to be easy. No one knows that better than I do. The time at your disposal is so desperately short. Unless you can foil this assassination attempt, President Tshombe could be dead in seventy-two hours, and all hell be let loose!

'The worst of it is,' the Belgian added, frowning, 'I can give you very little to go on. Basically, I've already told you all I know. A young Luvale, a black boy, brought me the first hint of this business.

I paid him to spy for me and to bring back more details, but — '

He shrugged, and his face set in hard and grim lines.

He said: 'The boy was murdered before he could give me any more information . . . hacked to pieces in an alley here in Elizabethville. That'll show you what we're up against, Mr. Brand.'

Brand moved in his chair. 'The police investigated?'

'After a fashion,' the Belgian said. He shrugged his shoulders again. 'In the present situation they're hard pressed to find enough men to maintain order in the city. They had none to spare to do a really thorough piece of detective work on the boy's murder. Their investigation — such as it was — produced no result.'

Brand nodded abstractedly.

He was looking into a wall mirror on the opposite side of the room, seeing the reflections of people coming and going. He pursed his lips thoughtfully. Two people had so far shown overweening curiosity about his arrival in Elizabethville — Angela De Villiers and the U.N. man,

61

O'Donovan. And the South African girl was sticking close to Cliff Wallace.

'Tell me,' he said to Van Cleve, where does Mr. Wallace come into this?'

'He knows you personally, Mr. Brand. I appealed to him to try to persuade you to take this assignment. With so much at stake and so little time I felt that you were probably the one and only man I'd ever heard of who could tackle this job with even the remotest chance of success. And I hope and pray that you are successful, Mr. Brand! We're all in your hands now. Everything depends on what you can do in the next seventy-two hours!'

'Then let's get started, shall we?' Brand leaned forward. He was brisk now. He was businesslike. 'Get your notebook out, Nick. Now, Mr. Van Cleve, I'll need to know all you can tell me about the men — and the women — closest to President Tshombe . . . '

* * *

The young man and the girl were standing close together at the bar as

Brand entered the lounge of the Hotel Livingstone after dinner.

Cornelius Van Cleve had left, and Nick had gone to his room.

Brand's gaze passed over the tables to the glittering array of bottles stacked behind the counter. The lighting in the room was warm and subdued.

The man and the girl standing at the counter were both white. The man had a lean and hungry look; a transatlantic haircut. He was young, and dark-haired, and he was dressed in the uniform of a corporal in the Canadian Army. He wore a United Nations armband, and he was slightly drunk. He was swaying on his feet and clutching a half-empty whisky glass in his hand as he declaimed loudly:

'It's gettin' men out here to this rotten, stinkin' country under false pretences that I'm not standin' for — I'm kickin' against it. I'm seein' the captain tomorrow. We volunteered for police duties out here, not blurry war service. Hell, I don't want to die out here. I got a lot of livin' and drinkin' in front of me yet. Some o' the natives in these parts are still in the

63

Stone Age. Some of them are cannibals. Some fight with bows and poisoned arrows.'

The soldier laughed: an ugly sound, without mirth.

'You know what else we've been told?' he asked the girl standing beside him. '"Remove the arrow within five seconds" — that's what we've been told. If you get it out in that time the poison only causes mild discomfort. That's what they say.'

Abruptly, he banged on the counter.

'Mild discomfort — hell!' he declaimed. 'What happens after the five seconds is up, that's what I want to know. I tell you, I'm fed up with it. I'm — '

The girl remained unimpressed. She said calmly: 'You're getting more money in pay and allowances out here than you've ever had in your life before.' Then she left him. He called after her: 'Hey, Crystal, honey — '

But the girl called Crystal had seen Brand, and she was moving towards him. She looked about eighteen, and her figure was slender and willowy under a severe two-piece business suit. She was a demure miss, Brand thought, watching her as she approached. A demure miss, with upswept bouffant-style raven black hair.

She reached him, and three-quarter-inch eyelashes fluttered. Delicate white hands fluttered, too. She said breathlessly; 'Oh, Mr. Brand, I recognised you right away, from your pictures. I'm English as well. It's wonderful to meet a fellow-countryman so far from home. Particularly such a world-famous one . . . '

There was light purple lipstick on her fragile mouth, and her perfume was subtle. She made an appealing figure, petite and helpless. But her violet eyes, Brand noted, were shrewd and calculating; the eyes of a young woman very experienced in the ways of the world.

He grew wary as she chattered on. At the bar, the young Canadian called loudly for another whisky. Simon Brand glanced briefly in his direction, and then eyed the girl called Crystal again. And he was suddenly very thoughtful.

The girl was touching his arm now

— fondling it almost. She was looking up at him very coquettishly. 'I just know I'll sleep more soundly tonight, Mr. Brand, with you here in E'ville. I just can't begin to tell you how wonderful it is to meet you . . . '

Simon Brand regarded her with a faraway look in his eyes. He remained distant; detached. His expression was enigmatic. She was very good, he thought, but she was overdoing it.

'Tell me — ' she began.

Simon Brand smiled. He didn't propose to tell her anything at all. But he spoke politely. 'It's been very pleasant meeting you, but now I really must go. I've an urgent appointment. I hope you'll excuse me. Perhaps we'll bump into each other again later.'

Gently, he detached her clutching hand from his arm. He moved on. He walked out of the lounge and out of the hotel, speed gathering in his stride. He went out into the dusky streets of Elizabethville, and he went quickly.

He really had no time to waste.

Cornelius Van Cleve had told him that

disaster threatened to engulf this state of Katanga inside the next seventy-two hours unless he, personally, could do something to stop it. And Brand didn't doubt that the Belgian had been speaking the truth.

But what could he do — until he knew all the facts? He was in no mood to dawdle. Seventy-two hours . . . so little time. He strode along the street purposefully.

He thought the first thing he must do was to learn something of the death of the Luvale black boy who had given Van Cleve his first hint of the violence and murder which threatened.

He thought that this — a call on the police — was the logical way in which to start.

6

Long Night

The girl called Crystal said, 'Damn!' She said it almost under her breath, but it was nonetheless explosive and vehement for that.

She stood in the centre of the polished parquet floor of the Hotel Livingstone's lounge, watching Simon Brand walk out on her.

'Damn!' she muttered again fiercely. 'Damn!'

It was a rare event in Crystal's life to have any man walk out on her. She didn't like it. Usually, her highly perfected brand of soft, appealing, feminine helplessness attracted men to her — not drove them away. Her mouth tightened briefly, expressive of her intense annoyance, but her brain was working quickly.

Simon Brand had walked out on her, but —

Perhaps his young partner, Nick Chandler would prove more susceptible to her technique . . . ?

The lean-and-hungry-looking Canadian had left the counter, and now he moved towards her unsteadily, whisky slopping over the rim of his glass. His smile was crooked; unpleasant. 'Tough luck, Crystal,' he murmured.

The girl turned on him sharply. She glared. Her violet eyes blazed with cold fury. Her breath hissed through her teeth. 'Get away from me, and keep away from me!' she spat at the United Nations man.

'But, Crystal — ' he began, drunkenly uncertain.

She slapped his face; viciously; hard. 'Get away from me! Right away!' The U.N. soldier backed off, one cheek burning red. He looked very angry; indignantly furious. But then he turned, downed his drink at a gulp, banged the empty glass on the counter, and stalked out of the lounge. He was so consumed by his blazing rage that, briefly, he didn't look drunk at all.

Breathing hard through delicate, dilated

nostrils, the girl called Crystal sat down at an empty table — only to get up again quickly. A fair-haired young man was coming in through the door.

Crystal composed herself — fast. Eyelashes fluttering, she descended on her new victim. She was demure again; fragile. Breathlessly she said: 'You're Mr. Chandler, aren't you? I'm so glad to meet you. Mr. Brand was telling me all about you and your assignment here. I was hoping that we might bump into each other. Mr. Brand had to leave in rather a hurry . . .'

Nick Chandler grinned. The girl looked nice, he thought. Very nice indeed. She was a petite little thing, with shimmering raven hair and a well-endowed figure.

But he didn't for one moment believe that his chief had told her anything at all of importance. He knew Brand better than that. So she was angling for information. Fine!

His own orders were to pick up whatever he could at the bar. And this girl might be worth picking up — if only for a short time. 'My friends call me Nick,' he admitted modestly.

She smiled. 'And I'm Crystal . . . '

Nick looked interested. 'That's an unusual name.'

'Isn't it?' She took a dainty step closer. Her subtle perfume reached out and touched him. 'It's a pet name, really. My mother came from Iceland.'

Nick reserved judgment, Crystal's accent was pure South Kensington. 'Can I get you a drink?' he asked. Just looking at this beautiful girl made his mouth dry.

'Why, thank you!' She laid a white hand on his arm. 'Though I don't drink as a rule. But, to please you . . . '

Nick turned to the Katangese barman and ordered a dry sherry for the young brunette; a Simba for himself. She sipped delicately, like a butterfly at nectar.

'Well, cheers,' said Nick and sank a couple of Simbas fast.

The local brew was strong. He told himself that he'd have to watch it — and that gave him an idea. She wanted him to talk, did she? Just how badly did she want to hear what he might have to say?

'Jolly good beer, this,' he said,' a little

too loudly, slurring his words. He very nearly missed the edge of the counter with his empty glass as he set it down. He had to fumble, thick-fingered to steady it and stop it falling.

'Jolly good beer,' he repeated, and swayed just a fraction. Crystal was opening a small handbag. It was stuffed with banknotes.

She said — hopefully — 'Of course, you'll have another?'

*　*　*

Simon Brand was talking to a senior police officer, named Glaubeck, in the gendarmerie headquarters in Elizabethville. The man was a Belgian; big, bull-necked, and powerfully built — though inclining somewhat to middle-aged fat.

However, he still looked tough. And at this moment, waiting for Brand to finish outlining his purpose in visiting police headquarters, he was also beginning to look rather impatient.

It was plain that he had much on his

mind, and that the police force in Elizabethville was currently very hard pressed.

For though Brand spoke quickly and the explanation of his purpose in coming here didn't take long, the telephone rang twice on the Belgian police officer's desk in that time and had to be answered on both occasions. Nor was this all.

Elsewhere in the big building, other telephones jangled incessantly. Squads of men clattered through the stone corridors, coming and going. Cars arrived in front of the headquarters and disgorged their occupants. Other cars pulled away. Activity was continuous.

Now the big Belgian police officer held up a hand.

'I am sorry,' said Glaubeck, 'but I have heard all I have time to hear, Mr. Brand. We are very busy here, you can see that for yourself. The presence of United Nations troops here in Elizabethville is fast making our jobs nearly impossible.

'Our people are being provoked all the time — Katangese, European, gendarmes and civilians alike. It has become very plain that the primary purpose of the United Nations here is to needle us into some sort of action. They seem determined to provoke us so that they can 'police' us and still appear to have clean hands in the eyes of the world. This my men and myself are working flat-out to prevent.'

His manner was brusque.

'I'm telling you this, Mr. Brand,' Glaubeck went on, 'so that you'll understand me when I say that the murder of one Luvale boy is of very small consequence to us here at this moment. I am being frank with you. I would be the first to agree that this state of affairs is regrettable, but — ' he shrugged, 'what can we do? We have only so many men at our disposal, and all of those are engaged in trying to keep our entire population calm and peaceful in the face of extreme provocation. We investigated the death of the Luvale boy, and, I will say it myself, the investigation was cursory.' He shrugged again. 'There the matter rests.'

Brand said: 'You found out nothing at all?'

Irritation creased the big Belgian's features. 'I have been trying to explain to you — ' he began.

Brand interrupted. 'Then the truth is that you did find out nothing.'

The police officer was clearly exasperated.

'Ach!' he growled. 'You are making this sound like the crime of the century! Believe me, it was far from being that!'

'The boy was still murdered,' Brand said.

'And I've told you why our investigation was sketchy. I admit it was sketchy, and I deplore it. But look — '

Brand interrupted again. 'You really have no idea at all who the murderer — or murderers — might be?'

'The boy was a Luvale,' the Belgian said very ungraciously. 'You appreciate the Luvales are the original tribesmen of Katanga? Well, with the spread of industrialism, the Balubas moved down from Kasai. And now there is no love lost between the two tribes. Consequently, I have little doubt that the boy's murderer was a Baluba and, as for motive, you'd find that in a quarrel over a girl, most likely. These things happen.'

'And whoever killed the boy gets away scot-free,' Brand said shortly.

'In the present circumstances — ' the police officer said exasperatedly 'I've told you — '

'Just the same, M'sieu Glaubeck,' Brand put in. 'I should appreciate your cooperation. I wish to investigate the dead boy's background, his home life and family, and his employer. And I haven't much time. I should also like to see the place where he was killed.'

The big Belgian policeman flushed angrily. He got out: 'Haven't you been listening to anything I've said? How can we give you any cooperation at all? We're desperately short of men! I — '

Brand said quietly; 'Mr. Van Cleve suggested that you would do your utmost to help . . . '

The man sitting on the other side of the scarred desk started to say something, thought better of it, then grunted and swallowed.

He said, 'Mr. Van Cleve . . . ? Cornelius Van Cleve?'

Brand nodded. 'That's right.'

'And you've just flown out here from London, you said?'

Brand nodded again, and the big Belgian's eyes narrowed. 'I knew he was interested in this business, of course . . . but not *that* interested. Oh, well, in that case . . . I suppose . . . '

Glaubeck leaned forward, and thumbed a bell-push on his desk. The name of Cornelius Van Cleve obviously carried considerable weight. To the tall, young Katangese gendarmerie sergeant who entered the room a moment later, the big Belgian said tonelessly: 'Henri — drop everything. You're to give Mr. Brand here a hand. Answer all of his questions. Take him wherever he wants to go. He's interested in that Luvale boy who was murdered. Help him all you can. Understand?'

The young Katangese sergeant looked quickly at Brand, and then nodded. '*Mais oui, patron.*'

Brand also spoke to the Belgian. He

said shortly: 'Thanks.'

Glaubeck didn't answer.

The Katangese sergeant opened the door, and ushered Brand out of the office. 'This way, m'sieu. Please come with me.'

And Brand went.

On the scarred desk behind him as he stepped into the corridor, the telephone started ringing again — insistently. But the big, middle-aged Belgian police officer didn't reach for it, didn't touch it. Not right away.

He let it ring a full minute. He was otherwise occupied. Eyes narrowed, hooded, and calculating, he first watched Brand all the way out of the room.

★   ★   ★

In the lounge of the Hotel Livingstone, Nick was still drinking Simbas, and apparently becoming more and more unsteady by the minute

'D'you work in 'Lizbethville?' he asked his attractive companion, thrusting his head forward practically into her face and regarding her owlishly.

'Yes,' the girl called Crystal told him. 'Here — ' she gripped his arm and helped him regain his balance as he lurched from one foot to the other. ' — here, you need another drink.'

'Was jus' goin' to get one,' Nick said indistinctly. He had drained his glass, and was making ineffectual passes at the bar with it, trying to put it down.

'My turn,' Crystal said, and she ordered. Nick struggled to light a cigarette. 'So ... so you work in 'Lizbethville, eh — ? Wadderyou do? Whatever it is, you're wasted ... nice girl like you ... '

'I'm only a private secretary,' she said.

Nick smiled broadly. 'I've always wanted a private secretary ... '

The conversation lapsed into banal innuendo.

★ ★ ★

The Katangese sergeant was pacing along the sidewalk beside Brand under the soft light of yellow street lamps.

'I'm Luvale too, *m'sieu*,' he told the

detective. 'Educated at Missionary School. The dead boy, Nsambo — he was of my tribe.'

'You knew him?' Brand asked.

'No, *m'sieu* . . . ' and then the Katangese sergeant grinned suddenly . . . ' but it would be fine to arrest some Balubas!'

They walked south along a broad avenue, past tall office blocks and shops. Brand smelt hibiscus and bougainvillea. There was garish colour and noise in the passage of big American cars. Somewhere, a radio blared jazz with undertones of Africa in its beat.

Brand glanced back suddenly, confirming a lurking suspicion. A taxicab followed slowly. It had been parked outside the police station. Now it was fifty yards behind.

Brand and the Katangese sergeant walked on.

Presently, the sergeant stopped. He pointed at a narrow alleyway between tall buildings. 'Nsambo was killed here, *m'sieu* . . . '

Brand stood poised in the dark, forbidding mouth of the alley. He glanced back over his shoulder. The cab had stopped, and a tall black got out.

Brand took a powerful electric torch from his pocket and sent the beam lancing into the alley. He followed it. 'Where does this lead?'

'No place, *m'sieu*,' the sergeant told him. 'Just to an empty lot. Mainly, I suppose it's just used as a short cut.'

Brand switched off his torch abruptly, and turned.

Back beyond the mouth of the alley, across the street, a man leaned against a wall, his face hidden behind the double-spread of a newspaper. A heavy man. Brand saw knife-edged, blue-grey gaberdine trousers, two-tone shoes slit at the sides, big splay feet. It would be easy enough for him to recognise the man again.

Satisfied that his follower was content to maintain a distant watch on him and no more, Brand searched the alley thoroughly, even though he had no expectation of coming across anything of value at this late stage. There was a doorway where a killer might have waited in hiding . . . he imagined the murdered boy hurrying along the alley all unsuspecting, the flash of a knife . . . the boy would have had no chance at all in such a confined space. Someone had planned well, he thought grimly; someone who knew the locality intimately.

He walked to the end of the alley, and saw rusting derelict cars dumped on a piece of wasteland. 'Did Nsambo live over this way?' he asked.

'No, m'sieu. He lived in the old town with his mother. I will take you there now.'

They retraced their steps, Brand and the Katangese sergeant. They came out on to the broad, well-lit avenue once again. And now Brand saw a balled newspaper in the gutter.

But of the man who had been following him, the big man with splay feet, there was no sign at all.

He had vanished.

* * *

Back at the Hotel Livingstone, Nick wore a vague expression. He seemed not completely in control of his faculties. His eyelids blinked heavily.

He swayed on his feet; was steadied. He yawned. 'Sleepy,' he announced. 'Goin' up . . . take a nap . . .'

Crystal's fragile, purple-coloured lips were close to his ear. She murmured, 'I'll come with you, darling . . . I've told you all about myself . . . now you can tell me all about yourself and your interesting work.'

She took his arm, and piloted him skilfully across the shining parquet floor. She led him towards the row of lift cages. Nick leaned on her. His feet traced an unsteady pattern. He looked stupefied . . .

The lift-cage rose swiftly, then stopped. The doors slid back. Holding on to his arm, Crystal guided Nick down a corridor. She produced a key and opened a door.

'Not my room,' Nick said tipsily.

'Of course it's your room, darling,' Crystal assured him, closing the door carefully behind her.

She did not put on the light. The

African moon shone through filmy curtains, revealing a long, low room. The girl pushed Nick gently, and his knees struck the edge of a divan, and he pitched forward.

As he struggled to sit up, he found the dark-haired Crystal beside him. Her arms slid round his neck, and her mouth sought his. She kissed him, and pressed herself hard against him. Then she kissed him again — urgently.

'Nice,' Nick murmured.

She snuggled closer.

'Yes, darling,' she said. 'But you have it in your power to make it nicer . . . '

* * *

Simon Brand and the young Katangese police sergeant were now beyond the limits of the broad, well-lit avenues. They moved through a maze of dark, narrow streets lined with drab dwellings. They were in the old part of Elizabethville.

The police sergeant threaded a way deep into the maze; the red-earth streets became dusty, winding lanes.

The dwelling houses became mere shacks of adobe and dark-burned brick covered with flat galvanised roofing, and in many places the zinc had worn away and the iron beneath turned to rust. This was the poor quarter — here the slums of the city. They carried a smell of neglect and squalor.

'Nsambo lived here, *m'sieu.*'

The sergeant paused at a half-open gate leading on to a cracked concrete path between straggling shrubbery. The path led up to a shanty set on its own. It was not a prepossessing residence.

Brand walked up the narrow concrete path. The shack was in darkness, and a foul greasy smell hung in the air. He rapped on the blistered door — and it swung open, creaking, before him. No sound came from within.

The sergeant called out in his own tongue, but there was no answer. The dark seemed to pulse with menace and, despite himself, Brand felt his heart beating faster and the hairs all the way down his back beginning to rise.

A choking atmosphere of evil came out

of the dark, silent shack. Brand had his Luger pistol hard in one hand. In the other, he had the torch he had used earlier.

Slowly, deliberately, almost dreading what he might see, he flashed the torch on.

And the young Katangese police sergeant standing beside him dragged in a sharp, involuntary breath as the light lanced into the dark room that lay open before them.

*   *   *

Nick lay on his back in one of the upper rooms of the Hotel Livingstone. The dark-haired girl called Crystal was close to him. Nick stretched. The taste of her lips and her warm breath was a pleasant memory.

'Now, darling . . . ' she leaned over him. 'We must know each other better . . . tell me about your job out here.'

Nick said vaguely, 'Yes . . . ' and yawned hugely. He said, 'Of course . . . '

Then he relapsed into silence again. Crystal waited. But Nick was breathing very heavily now. Suddenly, softly, he began to snore.

Crystal breathed hard, and she shook him. She shook him violently. Her voice pleaded. 'You can't go to sleep now, Nick — we're going to be friends, remember! This isn't fair!'

Nick's snores increased in volume.

Suddenly vicious, Crystal thumped a tiny fist on his chest. But Nick gave no sign of consciousness. She hit him again but he just lay like a resonant log.

Finally, in despair, she stood up. She stood over him; glared at him. 'Damn!' she said explosively. 'Damn and blast!'

She spun on her stiletto heels and went out of the room, slamming the door behind her.

Then Nick rose swiftly — not at all sleepy now. He crossed to the door and edged it open. He was in time to see Crystal disappear down a flight of stairs at the rear of the hotel. She seemed to be in a hurry.

Nick smiled to himself — and followed her.

The light from Simon Brand's torch illuminated a ghastly scene with stark clarity.

He saw a truckle bed in the centre of the floor of the adobe shack. He saw bedclothes torn this way and that; an overturned chair. He saw a huddled body on the dirty, scuffed and stained boards of the floor — the body of an old native woman, her face ugly in fear and in death.

She lay in a pool of blood on the floor, and the blood was still wet. Nor was this all. And now Brand could see for himself why the Katangese police sergeant had started to shiver beside him.

The arms and legs of the old woman's corpse ended in abrupt stumps. Both hands and feet had been crudely hacked off — and taken away like so much meat.

They were not with the brutally butchered corpse of the old woman.

They were nowhere in the room.

7

Men of Power

The dawn sky was a brilliant flamingo pink, and the white stone façades of the bungalows and office blocks in Elizabethville were veined with an ever-changing pattern of soft red light as Simon Brand returned to his hotel.

He was tired, and he was angry.

He felt sure that the mother of the Luvale boy, Nsambo, had known nothing of the plan to assassinate President Tshombe, yet she had been brutally struck down and her dead body savagely mutilated . . . and he thought he knew why.

His lips were drawn into a fine line as he entered the lobby of the Hotel Livingstone. All night he had been with the police, searching for clues, finding nothing. The killer had got clean away.

There was a clearly defined image in

his mind. An image of a heavy man with splayfeet and two-tone shoes slit at the sides; the black who had watched him search the alleyway where the boy Nsambo had died.

Brand wanted to meet this man again. He wanted that very much. He suspected that it was because he had been seen searching the alley and because he had so obviously been investigating the Luvale boy's murder that the old native woman, Nsambo's mother, had been brutally butchered too.

Someone was warning him to drop this case and clear out of Katanga. That was why . . .

He found Nick in the lounge of the hotel drinking black coffee. 'Any message for me?' he asked his young partner wearily.

'I wouldn't know, chief.' Nick shrugged. 'I haven't been back long myself. That English tramp, Crystal, picked me up — ' he smiled at the memory — 'and, afterwards, I tailed her home. She led me straight to a bungalow in the U.N. camp . . . and to

Declan O'Donovan! I understand from the staff here that she's his private secretary. But to my way of thinking that's . . . er . . . putting it politely. I waited around the bungalow for quite a while, but she didn't reappear. And the lights had gone out . . . '

Brand nodded absently. So the girl Crystal was working for the U.N. official, O'Donovan. Interesting . . . but right now he had something else on his mind. 'Come with me, Nick,' he said abruptly.

They went up in the lift: up to Brand's room. And the detective had no sooner opened the door than they could see that he had had a visitor during the night. Someone had left a small wicker basket for him. It stood on the carpet in the middle of the room. And it smelt — horribly.

Nick looked startled. 'What on earth —?'

Brand said: 'Get on to police headquarters at once. There's a senior police officer — a Belgian, a man called Glaubeck. I want him over here. Get him out of bed, if necessary. I want action on this!'

He flung back the lid of the wicker

91

basket, grimly expectant. And he saw exactly what he had expected to see . . .

Nick crowded nearer to look inside the basket — and put his hand over his mouth. Suddenly, he felt sick.

He was looking at a freshly severed pair of black hands, and a pair of severed black feet.

★   ★   ★

The big, burly Belgian police officer stood in Brand's room less than half an hour later, staring with distaste at the contents of the basket. 'You know what this means, M'sieu Brand?'

Brand nodded. His voice rang out harshly. 'Somebody doesn't want me investigating. It's a powerful hint to leave well alone.'

The big, burly Belgian called Glaubeck rubbed the back of his bull neck and grunted. 'So that's what you think . . . ' He prodded at the severed hands, brooded a moment. 'It's Baluba work. Ritual mutilation. We get plenty of reports of such atrocities in the fighting up north.

Reports of black — and white — hands dangling from the belts of the Baluba.'

'But Nsambo wasn't mutilated in this way, was he?' Brand said sharply.

'*Non, m'sieu* . . . ' the Belgian admitted.

'And the man I described for you — the man who followed me in a taxi to the alley where Nsambo was killed — Brand's voice was tense — 'any trace of him yet?'

Glaubeck sighed. 'Not so far . . . but we have identified him. His name is M'Polo, and he has a police record. A bad one. But — where to find him . . . ?' Broad shoulders shrugged. 'There are many rat-holes to swallow up such a one.'

'I want him found,' Brand said grimly. 'I want to question him personally.' He touched the side of the wicker basket. 'Will you be able to find out where this came from?'

'You mean — where it was made?' The big police officer shrugged again. 'It is unlikely. It is typical native work. You'll see hundreds of baskets exactly like this one on sale all over E'ville. There's nothing unusual about it.

'However,' Glaubeck went on, 'we should be able to get a description of the person who brought it here. Someone in the hotel must have seen him.'

Brand ran a hand over the stubble on his jaw. He felt very weary, yet he had never been more conscious of the fact that he could not — dare not — take his rest and relax. Van Cleve had told him that he had just seventy-two hours in which to stave off President Tshombe's assassination and the hellish nightmare of Lumumbist invasion and terror that would surely follow. A bare seventy-two hours — and that had been the deadline given him at dinner last night. Already ten of those hours had been spent. And what had they brought forth? Another monstrous, barbaric killing! A foretaste of the widespread slaughter to come — unless, somehow, he could prevent it.

There was so much to do, and so little time.

Simon Brand's eyes were cold as he looked at Glaubeck, the big Belgian police officer, and they were bleak. 'One thing's sure,' he said. 'I want results. And Mr. Van Cleve will back me in this — right up to the hilt. I want the man called M'Polo found, and I want the person who left this basket here traced. I want results, Captain Glaubeck, and I must have them. And I want them fast!'

* * *

Cliff Wallace, the London *Morning Post's* special correspondent in Katanga, was not altogether happy. But he should have been.

He was travelling in style, being driven in a shiny new emerald green Studebaker by one of the most beautiful blondes it had ever been his good fortune to meet. But . . .

He glanced sideways, taking in Angela De Villiers' profile — and what a profile! — as revealed by the taut, safari-style shirt that she wore. He ought to be happy, he argued. Most men would have given a great deal to be in his place. His mouth tugged down wryly. Clearly, some of them had. Obviously, the blonde

Angela couldn't run this car on a working journalist's expense account — not unless the accountants on South African papers were a very different breed from those penny-pinching shylocks in London.

A clue to his present unhappiness was hidden here.

This particular blonde was a journalist. A rival journalist. And Wallace wanted a scoop. So, professionally speaking, he didn't want Angela always hanging around him.

On the other hand, privately and personally, he couldn't see too much of her — and he had already seen quite a lot. Life could be very confusing, he decided.

He sighed.

The Studebaker convertible slid into the kerb, and then stopped. Angela De Villiers opened the door closest at hand, and swung her long, slim legs out. Wallace noted with a practised eye, just what a short skirt did for a woman, and brightened. He pushed his old felt hat on to the back of his head, and followed the blonde Angela on to the pavement.

They were in a select residential area of Elizabethville. The avenue was wide and tree-shaded. Exquisite scents floated from flowering shrubs laid out in neat rows on billiard-table lawns. The houses here were well on the way to being mansions. They were built of burnt brick and elegantly carved super-white stone. They looked very exclusive, and very expensive.

Wallace rested a hand on an ornamental, wrought-copper gate, and looked up at high windows winking in the sun like curious eyes. 'Well, blondie,' he said, and he sounded just a little reluctant, 'it seems like we've arrived.'

Angela smiled. She looked like a sleek, well-bred Siamese cat with one eye firmly fixed on a new-opened tin or delectable cream. She moved with a satisfied air, sure of herself. 'I keep telling you, Cliff darling,' she said sweetly, 'we can cover this interview together. As long as we both get our copy off at the same time, we won't compete with each other. We'll each have exclusives in the territory covered by our individual papers. So don't be pig-headed.'

Cliff Wallace had to agree with what she said. It was just that he automatically thought in terms of worldwide 'beats'. This was the way he'd been trained. 'Okay, okay,' he said. 'We'll do it together.'

They went up white stone steps between tall, slender columns, and Wallace rang a bell on the porch. Footsteps echoed across tile from the other side of the heavy door. When a black manservant appeared, Wallace flashed his Press card and said: 'Special correspondent, the London *Morning Post*. I have an appointment with Doctor Yoruba.'

Cornelius Van Cleve had arranged this interview for him, as a reward for persuading Brand to accept his assignment. Yoruba was an important man in Elizabethville, close to President Tshombe, and a source of reliable inside information.

' . . . And Miss De Villiers of the *Johannesburg Sun*!'

'You are expected, *m'sieu*.'

Cliff and Angela moved across a tiled

98

hall decorated with African shields and crossed assagais. They entered a large, airy room with suntrap windows, leopard skin rugs and Impressionist paintings, native beadwork and a cocktail bar.

Doctor Julius Yoruba advanced to greet them: a tall, handsome black, faultlessly dressed in a beautifully cut charcoal grey lounge suit.

But he was not alone in the room.

The European in the room with Doctor Yoruba was slightly-built; thin. He had a gaunt, hollow-cheeked face, a ginger spade beard, and immensely shaggy eyebrows.

He was dressed in a faded white-linen suit.

His expression gave the impression of a man withdrawn into himself: a man given to a lifetime of silent, intense introspection. But his brilliantly blue eyes came up sharp and alert at the entrance of Wallace and the beautiful Angela De Villiers.

Wallace knew of this man — Stephan Trois — and grew excited. This was a real stroke of luck! For if meeting and interviewing Doctor Yoruba was a terribly difficult thing for any journalist to achieve — and it was, unless one had the help of someone with considerable influence in Katangese government circles, like Cornelius Van Cleve — then to arrange to come face-to-face with this other man, Stephan Trois, was next door to being completely impossible.

Stephan Trois preferred to stay out of the limelight. So did Yoruba, too, for that matter. But it was known — definitely known — that Yoruba was one of President Tshombe's most respected advisers. On the other hand, nothing at all was definitely known about the part Stephan Trois played in Katangese politics. All was conjecture.

It was said that he was high in the President's confidence, and a man who knew more about palace intrigue than any other European living. He it was — it was rumoured — who sat in on the policy-making sessions of the Katangese government, and carried top secret instructions the length and breadth of the country.

A cosmopolitan, with a suggestion of Central European origin, he admitted to no nationality at all.

Wallace began to wonder just what Stephan Trois and Doctor Yoruba had been discussing before he came into the room . . .

Then Doctor Yoruba stepped forward, smiling, the glint of gold teeth in his mouth. 'Mr. Trois has just returned from the fighting area in the north,' he announced. 'Perhaps he may have news of some value to your papers.'

'That's fine,' Wallace said, and his voice died. Stephan Trois didn't seem to appreciate the *Morning Post's* gift to journalism. But Stephan Trois appreciated Angela De Villiers all right.

He was staring hard, inspecting the long-legged South African girl from the crown of her blonde head to the tips of her painted toenails, which peeped out from her black suede sandals. His brilliant blue eyes lingered over her.

'I'm very pleased to have the opportunity of meeting you, Miss De Villiers,' Trois said. 'Your — er — fame has reached my ears, even though I lacked an opportunity to meet you until this moment. Perhaps you will do me the honour of joining me for dinner this evening?'

Even Wallace — himself a fast worker — could hardly believe his ears. He felt an unreasoning flush of jealousy, a rush of protectiveness towards his blonde companion. Hell, he wouldn't trust this character with a female mamba . . .

He grunted. 'Let's get down to business, shall we?'

But, suddenly, Stephan Trois began to cough.

It was a desperate sound; a terribly hard and sick sound. And it swiftly increased in violence. Wallace and Angela both stared at the man aghast.

Stephan Trois coughed and coughed. His face went a leaden grey. He was gripped by a seizure, a terrible paroxysm, which doubled him up and finally left him sweating and feebly gasping and sawing for breath.

He sat down unsteadily, ashen-cheeked, while Yoruba quickly poured brandy. Hand wavering, he gestured for Yoruba to keep pouring until a large tumbler was filled to the brim.

Then, greedily, he seized the tumbler and held it tightly in both trembling hands — but only for an instant. Immediately and amazingly, he gulped the half pint of strong spirit straight down.

Wallace marvelled.

He had never heard a man cough like Stephan Trois outside the approaches to a graveyard. And he had never seen anyone down half a pint of strong brandy in something like two seconds flat and seem only the better for it. Trois looked as though he'd just been given a swift blood transfusion.

The colour flooded back into his gaunt and hollow grey cheeks. His sadly sagging red beard seemed to suddenly bristle again with new life. His palsied hands steadied. He set down the drained glass without a tremor and then — most surprising of all — proceeded to act as though the whole incident in its entirety had never happened. He didn't refer to it.

He ignored it. He didn't even thank Yoruba for his timely offer of the brandy. Instead, calmly leaning forward in his chair, he touched the engraved silver belt encircling Angela De Villiers' waist. 'Delightful . . . fascinating workmanship!' he murmured, as though nothing had intervened to interrupt their conversation. He lifted his brilliantly blue eyes to the girl's face. 'I'm sure that we must have many interests in common.'

Angela De Villiers had been regarding him somewhat uncertainly, plainly more than a little alarmed by the terrible coughing fit that had seized him. But now, as though in answer to some compulsive cue in his soft-murmured words, she parted orange lips in a dazzling 'come-on' smile.

A conditioned response, Wallace found himself thinking bitterly, jealously, and very unkindly. What a woman! Pavlov would have been interested in her. She would have made a change from his dogs.

She said provocatively: 'Perhaps we'll discover how much we have in common tonight, Mr. Trois. I'll be happy to accept your invitation.'

So now she gets an exclusive, Wallace thought sourly, and scowled. The hell with women reporters!

Julius Yoruba interrupted. 'I think Mr. Wallace is getting impatient, Stephan. It is time to begin . . . '

Yoruba was possibly the most handsome black Wallace had ever seen. His build was solid, and he exuded charm — but not in any nauseous way. His skin was dull as old ivory; dry. The gold teeth glinted again. 'Perhaps you would like to start, Stephan?'

The other man nodded.

Then, much to Wallace's surprise, he fished a thin, black and strong cheroot from his pocket, and bit off one end of it. The journalist's eyebrows climbed. He thought that if he had a cough like the one Trois had got he certainly wouldn't be smoking. But . . . he shrugged mentally, it wasn't *his* funeral. He leaned forward and snapped his cigarette lighter.

Trois glanced at it, then shook his head.

'Thank you — no,' he said briefly. 'I can't stand petrol fumes. They make me choke.'

He struck a match and dragged on the cheroot with evident enjoyment. Then he blew out a cloud of villainously yellow smoke that made Wallace's eyes burn.

★ ★ ★

Stephan Trois concluded abruptly ' . . . and so there's fighting going on around Manono, four hundred miles north of E'ville, a small tin-mining town. It began when a Lumumbist force moved down from Kivu . . . and the U.N. patrols allowed them through! There's a lot of Baluba in that area, and they're hostile to President Tshombe. Now they're claiming to have set up a new province they call Lualaba.'

He tugged at his ginger spade beard, pulled at his cheroot; his gaze settled steadily on Angela De Villiers' waist belt, on the nymphs and satyrs and Pan playing his flute.

'Our Katangese gendarmerie mined the bridges leading south,' he continued, 'and our aircraft have bombed Manono. But the outcome is not yet certain. The Baluba, stimulated by drugs, captured some of our men and tortured them to death. They also wiped out an Irish U.N. patrol. It's a three-cornered fight and losses have been severe . . . and a platoon of Katangese European troops was in a clash with U.N. forces.'

Wallace, hat on knees, scribbled furiously. He said: 'What's the official reaction to all this?'

Doctor Yoruba interposed smoothly. 'The President has quite rightly denounced the United Nations for allowing Communist troops to invade our country — a mutinous act by the traitor Gizenga. There is much bad feeling in the Palace — naturally. Tempers are rising. Fortunately Moise Tshombe is a strong man . . .'

The voice of Yoruba held awe and reverence. His tone implied that the President was the only man who could save Katanga. And in this, Wallace thought, he was probably right.

'President Tshombe has said that the entire Katangese population — both black and white — will be mobilised to face this unprovoked declaration of war! We shall take to arms against the United Nations itself if necessary. The President has called on the people of Katanga to resist to the death. You must know, Mr. Wallace, that the behaviour of some of the U.N. troops here has been scandalous . . . assaulting our women . . . looting shops.'

Indignation deepened his voice.

'The Ethiopian contingent in particular — they are no more than brigands in uniform. Some are common criminals given a choice between long terms of imprisonment or joining the U.N. forces. As a result, President Tshombe has banned contact with the United Nations delegation here, both military and civil. The announcement will be made public within the next few hours.'

Wallace could contain himself no longer. He jammed his hat on his head and grabbed Angela's wrist. 'Come on,' he said urgently. 'We've got to get this on the wires . . . '

They left the room of contemporary furniture and native carvings: a room where the ancient horn of Africa met industrial Europe. And who could say which would assimilate the other?

* * *

As the door closed behind Cliff Wallace and Angela De Villiers, Stephan Trois crushed out his half-smoked cheroot. He crashed it out with brutal, unnecessary force and turned sharply on Doctor Yoruba, his gaze as flat and as deadly as that of a basilisk.

'What the devil are you playing at, Julius?' he demanded. 'Why did you tell those damn reporters all that?'

Doctor Julius Yoruba was not intimidated. 'Have a care, Mr. Trois,' he said softly. 'I am not one of your 'monkeys' to be ordered around. And I, too, have the President's ear.'

Trois gave a short, sharp and unpleasant laugh. 'That's only because he doesn't know you're a Baluba. If he did, he'd have your ears — both of 'em!'

The mask of Julius Yoruba slipped a fraction. Under the veneer of civilization, the savagery of old Africa welled up like a mamba about to strike. 'Perhaps we both have secrets to hide,' he suggested, 'If the President knew . . . '

They faced each other, tense, toe-to-toe, the black and the white. Two powerful men — stalemated.

Stephan Trois laughed again. This time it was a much easier sound. 'In that case, we'd better remain friends, Julius.'

Yoruda emptied what remained of the bottle of brandy into two glasses, He handed one glass to Trois. 'To friendship,' he said, mildly ironical.

They drank the toast, clinking glasses. Again, Trois took the brandy straight down in a gulp.

Both men smiled; deadly, false smiles.

For neither had the least doubt of what was in the other's mind. Each knew the other's thoughts and intentions.

There was no trust between them — none at all.

8

Night in Elizabethville

The living room of Declan O'Donovan's bungalow had an air of abandoned luxury. It was implicit in the carelessly strewn silks; in the reek of heavy perfume; in the rich red drapes covering the windows. The room of the United Nations' official had a voluptuous air; an air of corruption.

The raven-haired girl called Crystal sat drinking gin. She had a glass in her hand and a bottle by her side, and as soon as the glass was empty she filled it again. There was nothing of the butterfly sipping nectar about her now. She was drinking hard. She was no longer 'eighteen and demure'. Every day of her age showed. And so did her sensuality.

In place of her severe two-piece business suit, she wore a silk wrap that lay carelessly open and revealed the provocative lines of her body. It revealed more. The change of dress revealed her true character. She had nothing to hide from Declan O'Donovan of the United Nations.

She watched the thin, intense man with sandy hair as he paced worriedly back and forth across the thick carpet. 'Oh, stop it, Declan!' she protested finally, 'You're getting on my nerves!'

Angrily, O'Donovan wheeled on her, his eyes filled with a surging animosity. 'If you hadn't bungled the job, Crystal — !' His voice was high. 'I can't afford to have anything go wrong at this stage! I must know what Brand is up to! How can I make plans when — '

She interrupted him. She patted the seat beside her. She purred placatingly, 'Stop worrying, darling. Come here . . . and relax.'

He flared at her, 'I'm not in the mood. You think you've got the cure for everything.'

Crystal's eyes hardened.

She said, suddenly spiteful, 'Whatever

it is that I've got certainly kept you on easy street in New York for some months — if you remember.'

And she laughed, a brittle sound.

She said, 'I must have been crazy to fall for that line of yours!' She mimicked his soft Irish brogue. 'Be nice to him, darlin' . . . he'll give you a present, and we need the money . . . ' She said, 'And how you got *this* job I'll never know — unless, unbeknown to myself, I earned it for you . . . '

There was too much truth in what she said. O'Donovan's teeth bared in an angry white line. He rounded on her; stood over her. He would have hit her. But at the last minute, a shrill voice in his brain counselled caution — and calm.

He had to control himself. He couldn't afford to make an enemy of Crystal. He still needed her. Somehow, he managed to force an uneasy laugh.

'You always were a great kidder, Crystal,' he said. 'Sure you helped out in New York, and I was — and am — very grateful. But can't we forget it? Those times are over. What you did in

New York . . . well, it's different now. But this bit of business has to go off right, with no hitches.'

He gestured round at the luxuriously appointed room.

'Unless this business goes right,' he said, 'how am I going to get the money for this kind of living for you? And — ' he continued quickly, as she made to speak — 'don't throw New York in my face again . . . please . . . '

He had to change his line of attack, and he knew it.

He moved closer; sat down beside her. He said, 'I was out of luck in New York until this job came along.' He said it soberly, and he managed to sound very sincere. 'And luck wasn't the only thing I was out of, honey. I must have been out of my mind, the things I asked you to do . . . '

He slid an arm around her. Deftly, with a kind of easy and persuasive professionalism, he gently stroked the erogenous zone at the nape of her neck.

He murmured, 'I love you, Crystal . . . you know that. I'm ashamed of the things I've asked you to do. But everything's changed now. Just so long as this bit of business goes right, we're not going to have anything to worry about any more . . . you and me. No, not ever. We're both going to be on easy street from now on . . . '

He thought he knew exactly how to handle this girl. Experience — and not only of Crystal — had taught him the things that women most wanted to hear.

His breath was warm on her neck, a sensuous tingling. 'I love you, honey . . . '

At this moment she would have done anything for him.

He murmured, 'We're going to be rich . . . '

He was speaking her language.

Crystal was a girl who appreciated luxury. She had been born in a Paddington slum. Her earliest memories were of war shortages and of rain leaking through a bomb-damaged roof. Her father had failed to return from France at the time of Dunkirk. Her mother had circulated from one American soldier to another . . . and Crystal had soon 'got the message'. At that time, the Yanks were the ones with the money.

This had been the first lesson she'd learned. After that, she'd quietly and avidly lapped up the rest. She'd soon graduated in the school of life — and with some kind of doubtful distinction.

She'd been extremely well-developed, but just sixteen years of age — and she'd been carrying her birth certificate in her handbag to prove it — when she'd gone hunting work in the West End, as a photographers' model. The following day had seen her installed in her own South Kensington flat. She'd never got around to doing any modelling. There had been no need. And, after that, in her own way and apart from a recent and rather disastrous interlude in America, she'd never looked back.

She had flown to America with a British television impresario who had promised her the big time and the bright lights. But things had gone wrong. The British impresario's method of introducing her to New York show business big-shots had been to encourage a strictly personal rather than a strictly business approach, and the result had been a surprise late-night visit from a couple of hulking members of the New York Vice Squad — which could have had the very unpleasant consequences of unsavoury publicity and prison if Crystal had not kept her head.

Even as it was, it was not a night she cared to remember in any detail.

The New York show business mogul she'd been entertaining had been encouraged to leave, and he had been glad to. And he must have tipped off the British television impresario, for no one else had come near the East side apartment all the night long. But Crystal herself had been compelled to stay.

Then, in the grey light of dawn, after the policemen had gone, she had packed her bags and skipped the apartment, too — in a hurry. She had been certain that the Vice Squad men, or their friends, would be back.

All that day, she had trudged the streets of New York until, in the evening, resting her aching feet in a downtown bar, she had picked up Declan O'Donovan.

He was not the first man she could have picked up, and he was not the most affluent-looking, or handsome. But Crystal had to have someone to feed her and to give her shelter, and the big thing in Donovan's favour that night was that, although he was obviously interested in her, he wasn't eyeing her in the usual woman-hungry way.

Crystal had, in fact, thought that he might be a man who would be kind to her for her own sake: that he wouldn't be too demanding. And in one respect, she could tell herself now, she had been right. It wasn't for himself that Declan O'Donovan had been greedy for favours — at least, not directly.

But, thank heaven, she thought, that phase hadn't lasted too long. Somehow and somewhere, Declan had picked up this job with the United Nations and brought her out here to Elizabethville. And now it looked like tough times could really be on the mend.

Holding her now, fondling her, Declan O'Donovan said it again — a reassurance.

'Believe me, Crystal, we're going to be rich . . . '

It was something she could not hear too often.

Her violet eyes glowed.

She let her empty glass fall on the thick carpet as his arm tightened around her compulsively. 'That's right, darling,' she said. 'Now — relax. The game's not over yet. If you get all het up you'll be no good for anything . . . '

★   ★   ★

The night was dark, with cloud blotting out the stars. Black shadow hung over the United Nations encampment just outside Elizabethville. A few lights glimmered from the bungalows.

In dark shadow, Simon Brand hugged the wall of Declan O'Donovan's bungalow, listening at the darkened window. A humourless smile tugged at the corners of his mouth and he touched Nick's arm. 'All right . . . they're pretty occupied . . . keep a lookout.'

'Right, chief.'

Brand glided silently along the length of the bungalow. He had already decided that the long low building was divided into two parts: one half office, the other half living quarters. He knew O'Donovan and Crystal were not in the office.

A thin-bladed knife appeared in his hand. He set to work on a window-catch. O'Donovan had set Crystal to pump him and Nick, and he wanted to know why. He needed to know urgently. Twenty-four hours of the bare seventy-two that he had to get results in this case had gone by, and he hadn't progressed very far. The thought worried him.

Unless he achieved something soon, President Tshombe was going to be killed and all varieties of hell let loose throughout Katanga. He desperately needed to make some positive progress in this investigation. As a start, he urgently needed to know what O'Donovan had to hide.

It had not been easy slipping past the wire and the sentries to enter the U.N. camp undetected — but Nick had known just where to make the breakthrough . . .

The window-catch sprung. Brand eased open the window and gently pulled back the curtain. There was darkness beyond. He climbed stealthily through, silently drew the curtain again, and blinked his flashlight. He'd guessed right; this was Declan O'Donovan's office. He saw a desk, a covered typewriter, a steel safe. It was a spartan office, and would not take long to search.

Brand crossed to the communicating door, and put his ear to it. He heard distant heavy breathing; a throaty laugh. He nodded to himself, grimly satisfied. O'Donovan would not be interrupting him.

He went through the desk drawers, scanning the paper that they contained. All routine stuff. Then he gave his attention to the safe in the corner of the room. It was small; a standard model. Brand went to work with a picklock, felt the tumblers click into position. He swung the steel door silently open.

There was a cashbox, and it held rather a lot of loose cash for a U.N. official to have. This might be money O'Donovan didn't want to pass through a bank. Brand wondered if the Irishman had a second source of income. Certainly, maintaining Crystal would be expensive.

There were box files that held Brand's attention but briefly. More routine papers.

And there was a bulky, sealed envelope, addressed to U.N. Headquarters at Leopoldville. Brand hesitated a moment, weighing the envelope in his hand, then he shrugged. In for a penny, in for a pound ... he broke the seal on the envelope and extracted the contents.

After that, a frown creased his forehead. He read slowly, carefully. This was important.

And, as he read, his face darkened. His expression grew bleak.

The document he held in his hand was a detailed plan for a United Nations' invasion of Katanga in force.

★　★　★

Miss Angela De Villiers, of the *Johannesburg Sun*, crossed her elegant legs and fitted a cigarette into a long green jade holder. She snapped an engraved silver lighter, and held the flame to her cigarette. She inhaled deeply.

On the opposite side of the room, Stephan Trois sighed quietly but persistently for a long moment, and then sat, still and silent, watching her. Finally Trois said: 'I can admire a woman with poise. And you've got plenty of that. In fact, my dear, you've got everything.'

The South African girl smiled, a contented-cat smile. She thought she had the situation well in hand . . .

Trois had dined her well in his private apartment a few miles outside the centre of Elizabethville. His conversation had been light and unexpectedly amusing. A black manservant had wheeled away the trolly table. Now they relaxed, just the two of them, in Stephan Trois' well-appointed living room.

The room told Angela De Villiers a lot about Trois. Its neatness revealed a meticulous mind. There was a box of thin black cheroots and three bottles of brandy on a glass-covered bookcase; and most of the books had a bearing on the Congo, its history, its peoples, and its resources. There were no pictures in the room.

To one side, near windows, was a long couch. On the other side of the room was a single, deep and comfortable armchair. There were no rugs to clutter the highly polished woodblock floor in between.

This was the room of a man living and working in the present time and place; a man impatient of fripperies and frivolities. A man with a direct approach to life — and to women.

Angela De Villiers knew what was coming. She knew the way that Stephan Trois' mind worked. And she was ready to do her own bargaining. She struck first.

'I'm a reporter, Mr. Trois. I'm here in Elizabethville to cover news and personalities. And you've a very interesting personality — a man of power and influence, I'd like material on your background and your life for a profile.'

One shaggy ginger eyebrow lifted in the face of the man opposite her. Stephan Trois was amused by her own direct approach. He said: 'I suggest an exchange of information, Miss De Villiers. I've been away from E'ville for some time, as you know, and there are things I'd like to try to understand — '

'Such as?' she prompted.

'I hear that Simon Brand arrived here yesterday.' The voice of the cosmopolitan was casual, but his gaze never left her face. Unblinking brilliant blue eyes almost hypnotized her. 'A good man, this Brand,' he murmured. 'I've heard stories about him, read about him in the newspapers. Just what is his purpose in coming here, to Katanga? Do you know?'

'I wish I did!' the South African girl sighed. 'But that man's as tight as a clam. I can't get an unguarded word out of him.'

'You can't have tried,' Trois said dryly.

'I know one thing,' Angela said. 'I know that it was Cliff Wallace, the *Morning Post* man, who persuaded him to come out here. And that's all I do know — except that as soon as Brand arrived Wallace introduced him to Cornelius Van Cleve.'

'Van Cleve, eh . . . ?' Trois' voice hardened momentarily. A brooding expression moved over his face. Then he relaxed again. 'That's interesting . . . '

'About yourself now, Mr. Trois — '

Stephan Trois was evasive. He tugged at his red spade beard, and he gestured. 'I don't appreciate people who dig into *my* past,' he said.

'I thought this was going to be an exchange of information,' Angela De Villiers objected. 'That's what you said.'

'Oh . . . oh, all right then . . . if you must write something about me . . . ' He shrugged. 'Oh, say that I was born somewhere in Europe, and call me an adventurer, if you like.'

A spark of humour showed in his brilliant blue eyes for an instant.

'Call me 'a citizen of the world',' he said. 'That may not be particularly favourably received by your own South African paper, but it'll go down very well with most sections of the British Press — if your profile is syndicated that far.'

Angela De Villiers smiled. Then she said, 'And that's all you're going to tell me about yourself?'

And Stephan Trois nodded.

'Then tell me about Julius Yoruba.'

'Yoruba . . . ?' Trois tugged at his spade beard again. 'He's a fanatic, I'd say. Africa for the Africans, and the greatest thereof is Moise Tshombe. A dedicated man, not like me. Oh — that is something else you can tell your readers. I'm here strictly for the money.'

Angela De Villiers regarded him quizzically, and then shook her head slowly. 'I'm not sure that that's true . . . '

Then she said: 'The authorities are cagey about allowing reporters into the bush — ' She moved over to the long couch, sat down again, and slowly crossed one silk-clad leg over the other. She made the movement with deliberation, careful not to dislodge the ash on the tip of her cigarette. The short white skirt she was wearing inched upwards. She murmured, 'It seems we reporters are indispensable to the bars of Elizabethville. Or something.'

'It's quite true that you, personally, are indispensable, Miss De Villiers,' Stephan Trois said. 'Or so I hear.' He looked avidly at her as she leaned back casually on the deep couch. He edged is own chair nearer. His hands were restless.

'But you could arrange it for me, Mr. Trois,' Angela urged. 'Your word carries some weight in official quarters. I want a trip into the interior — somewhere near the fighting, so I can get a good story. A really big story. What is happening here in Katanga — so close to South Africa's frontiers — is of vital interest to my paper's readers.'

Trois was not impressed. 'Too dangerous,' he said, shaking his head.

'Dangerous — phooey! Who are you kidding?' She kept at him; this was what she wanted — just as she certainly knew what he wanted. A bargain would be struck. She said, 'I know you can fix it for me.'

'Perhaps . . . ' he said now. His eyes roved over her. 'But I think it could be a pity if anything unpleasant happened to you. A shocking waste!'

'But you will arrange the trip for me?' she persisted. Her eyes were bright.

He regarded her thoughtfully for a very long moment.

Then — 'Very well,' he said. 'If you're so set on it.' He shrugged his shoulders. 'It's your life. You should know what you're doing.'

His manner now became brisk and decisive.

'I'll lay on a car and a driver for you,' he said. 'I'll lay them on for tomorrow morning — early. But I insist, that you don't travel alone. Take someone else — another European with you. Perhaps that *Morning Post* correspondent . . . what's his name . . . Wallace? Yes, if you take Wallace with you, and the native driver . . . '

Angela made a face. 'I'd rather that the escort you're insisting on wasn't another reporter,' she said. 'But thanks anyway. It's very good of you. And I'm very grateful . . . '

Slowly Trois got to his feet. Now he stood over her, looking down, and there was something tense and demanding in the way he regarded her.

'Grateful . . . ?' he echoed. 'Just *how* grateful are you, Miss Villiers? That's a question I'd like answered here and now.'

9

Journey into Terror

Wallace said angrily, 'I'm not letting you go, Angela, and that's flat! The bush is no place for a woman!'

The blonde South African girl smiled at him. 'I didn't know you cared, Cliff.'

They stood on the steps outside the Hotel Livingstone in the warm morning sunlight, waiting for Stephan Trois' promised car. Angela De Villiers looked unconcerned. Wallace's square face was serious. He was alarmed for her. He had heard reports of mutinous and hostile tribesmen. Reports that didn't bear thinking about.

'Let me go alone, Angela. I'll fill you in with the copy when I get back.'

She remained stubborn. 'It was my idea in the first place, Cliff — and I'm going. You wouldn't be coming at all if Stephan Trois hadn't insisted!'

Cliff Wallace began, 'And that's another thing! How did you manage to persuade — '

Then a powerful black Armstrong Siddeley limousine swept across the Place de l'Etoile and stopped by the steps outside the hotel. A dark face grinned at them from behind the wheel. 'Mamselle De Villiers and M'sieu Kirby?' the black driver asked. 'I'm sent by M'sieu Trois.'

Wallace said, 'We ought to let Brand know — '

But Angela was impatient. She made herself comfortable in the back seat and held the door open for him. 'Why?' she demanded. 'Trois has arranged everything. Are you coming or not?'

Wallace sighed. He climbed in beside her. Angela De Villiers was a woman on whom argument was completely wasted. 'I hope you know what you're doing,' he grumbled.

The black driver wore a chauffeur's uniform and peaked cap. He slammed the door on them, and slid back behind the wheel.

He was a big man, heavy on his feet and the two-tone shoes that he wore and which jarred with the rest of his uniform were slit at the sides for the sake of comfort.

The big black Armstrong Siddeley roared away at high speed, heading out of Elizabethville.

★ ★ ★

Simon Brand was running an electric razor over his face before breakfast. He stood near a window in his room at the front of the Hotel Livingstone, glancing out over the Place de l'Etotie. Early morning sunlight warmed the white stone arcades; the pungent scent of eucalyptus hung in the air.

Simon Brand's mood was a tense one. He was terribly conscious of the all-too-swift passage of time. Much had to be done if he was going to save President Tshombe from assassination. He was thinking about Declan O'Donovan and the invasion plan he had found in the Irishman's safe. O'Donovan would have to be watched very narrowly, he thought. A job for Nick.

And that was the moment when he saw a big, black Armstrong Siddeley limousine swing across the plaza and pull up in front of the hotel.

Seconds later, he saw Angela De Villiers and Cliff Wallace step into the car, and he frowned.

If they were going out of town on a trip . . . still, perhaps someone else knew where they were going . . .

Then he saw the uniformed chauffeur slam the door on them. And, after that, events moved at lightning speed. For Brand not only saw that the man was big, broad and heavy, he also saw his shoes — two-tone shoes, slit at the sides. And big splay feet.

It was enough. Recognition was instant. This was the black man who had watched him search the alley where the Luvale boy had been murdered. This was the man he badly wanted to question, both in connection with the first brutal murder and the second — the savage slaying of the Luvale boy's mother.

This man was M'Polo! Brand jerked into action.

He lunged for his shoulder holster, rammed his Luger into it, grabbed up his jacket. He threw the holster on, and buckled it up at a run. He burst into Nick's room to find his young partner was still only halfway through washing and shaving, and only half-dressed.

'M'Polo,' Brand rapped. 'I've just spotted him. And I'm going after him. I want you to sit on Declan O'Donovan's tail and see if he contacts anyone.'

Then he ran.

He didn't wait for the lift. He took the stairs three at a time, and lunged across the hall and down the stone steps to the street.

The Armstrong Siddeley had vanished.

That didn't worry Brand. He had noted the direction in which the car was facing, and there was only one main road for it to take.

But there wasn't another available car in sight . . .

He dived through the arcade alongside the Livingstone, to reach the hotel's garage. Angela De Villier's green Studebaker convertible was the car nearest the doors of the garage, and it wasn't locked. Brand jerked in behind the wheel, whipped the ignition wires out from under the dashboard, and twisted them together.

Then he gunned the Studebaker's engine and rocketed out of the garage in the direction that the Armstrong Siddeley had taken — in swift pursuit.

★ ★ ★

The black Armstrong Siddeley carrying Wallace and Angela De Villiers moved fast.

It was big and powerful.

It surged out of Elizabethville, heading north.

There was hardly any traffic on the road at this early hour, and the big black driver hogged the centre of the wide, dead-straight way. Suburbs flashed past; neat rectangular houses with diamond-shaped flowerbeds, homes of employees of the Union Meniere.

They glimpsed President Tshombe's palace; the tall smokestack of some distant smelting plant; the stepped clay banks of a long-exhausted copper mine; a mountainous heap of black slag. The road continued smooth and straight. Once it curved briefly round a massive anthill — then ploughed straight on again. The Armstrong Siddeley continued to accelerate.

In the back of the car, Wallace turned to the blonde Angela with a crooked grin on his rugged face. 'This boy's good,' he murmured. 'I don't know where we're going, but we're going to get there real fast!'

And he laughed.

Wallace had lost his doubts about the wisdom of making this trip. A feeling of excitement was lodged deep inside him now. Maybe, this time, he was really on to a big story — at least Angela seemed to think so.

He looked again at the blonde South African girl sitting beside him. Her skirt had crept up above her knees. Wallace let one hand drop lightly on to sheer nylon.

He squeezed the knee beneath the nylon affectionately.

'Lay off, Cliff,' Angela said in a bored voice. 'It's too early in the day for that.' And she tucked her long legs beneath her.

Wallace remembered her dinner date with Stephan Trois. That was how they'd come to be on this trip. Bet she didn't talk to him in that cool voice, he thought sourly. He lit two cigarettes; passed one to her.

He was thoughtful. 'Angela, when this assignment is over, why don't you pull up stakes? Why go back to South Africa? You could come back to London with me, and I'm pretty sure I could fix you up with a job on the *Post*. South Africa's future is dicey. There's bound to be big trouble there sooner or later.'

Wallace's blonde companion raised an eyebrow, amused.

'South Africa suits me fine,' she said. 'I'm not thinking of making a change. As for the country's future, I think you're too pessimistic. We'll get by — if only outsiders will leave us alone, and let us sort out our problems in our own way.'

137

'I still think you'd be better off in London,' Wallace said. 'Look at it this way. You — '

'The answer's 'no', Cliff,' Angela said firmly, and Wallace sighed, shrugged, and relapsed into silence.

The broad arrowing road sloped downhill now. The Armstrong Siddeley gathered even more speed. It seemed as though it might become airborne any second. It fairly flashed over the ground.

It tore past two black cyclists travelling in the opposite direction. The funnel of a wood-burning stern-wheeler glinted briefly from the direction of the river, like a silver mast half-hidden by vivid green foliage. And then, suddenly, directly ahead, a roadblock leapt into view.

Wallace swore.

The roadblock was manned by heavily-armed troops of the United Nations. The familiar and distinctive blue steel helmets were clearly visible. So were two soundly-constructed machine-gun emplacements. Big signs shrieked '*Halt!*' in six languages. 'This looks like the end of the line,' Wallace fumed.

He said: 'It's odds-on these monkeys won't let us pass! So bang goes our trip to see the fighting up north. Bang goes a rattling good story. They'll turn us round and send us back to Elizabethville.'

But things didn't work out that way.

It would have been better, much better, for Wallace and Angela if they had — if the roadblock had stopped them. Then they would have been spared the torment and horror which fate had in store.

'Here we go,' grumbled Wallace, as the big Armstrong Siddeley got to within three hundred yards of the roadblock and began to slow down. 'Now these U.N. monkeys give us the run around. Now we're turned back!'

But it didn't happen.

For, the next instant and without warning, the Armstrong Siddeley's black driver took the big car clean off the road altogether in a wide, bucking swerve. It charged across red earth to reach a distant cart track. It bypassed the roadblock. It left it behind.

U.N. soldiers waved their arms wildly, and shouted. The car hit rocks and bumps and jolted shudderingly. Someone back at the roadblock started shooting. And a bullet whanged into the big car's body. But it did not stop.

'Great! That's the stuff!' Wallace crowed. 'What a driver!'

He was exultant, and so was Angela.

They should have been down on their knees, saying a prayer.

They didn't know — didn't dream — that their driver was a dedicated killer.

★ ★ ★

Now a semi-barren waste of desert spread out on either side of the Armstrong Siddeley. Dust sprayed up from the wheels of the car, a reddish pall that hung in the air behind them, marking their passage. Now the rough cart track they travelled began to twist and wind.

They flashed past jagged rocks, sharp and pointed like needles. They saw a lonely wooden shack stuck out in the middle of nowhere, with scrawny vegetation and grey-white boulders glinting with mica all around.

On and on the black limousine surged, eating up the miles, the powerful engine racing flat out. As the sun climbed higher, the back of the car became an oven, hazy with tobacco smoke.

Angela said: 'Let's have a window open, Cliff, for heaven's sake! Let's have some fresh air!'

'Right!' Wallace said. He tried the window on the side of the car's rear compartment. It wouldn't move. 'Jammed,' he muttered. 'That bullet must have done it.' And he leaned across her, smiling wolfishly. It was not unpleasant to lean across Angela.

But the window on her side wouldn't open either . . .

Wallace frowned. He rapped on the solid glass partition that isolated them from the driver. The big man took no notice. The car surged forward, weaving at high speed. Wallace rapped on the glass harder . . . and now the driver turned his head.

They saw a dark face with teeth parted in a broad grin. But the eyes mocked them silently. There was infinite cruelty and menace in the man's exultant expression. Then he turned his head away again, and concentrated on his driving.

A chill needled Wallace's spine.

It was baking hot in the Armstrong Siddeley's enclosed rear compartment, but Wallace broke out in a cold sweat. 'There's something very wrong here,' he said abruptly. 'Looks like we've walked right into trouble!'

He tried to open the door on his side of the car. It was locked.

Angela was wrestling with her door. 'Locked too,' she said in a voice that momentarily threatened to climb out of control. 'Windows and doors — they're all locked, Cliff!'

Wallace looked grim. 'We've got to do something — '

Angela showed him what to do. Perhaps she'd had experience of locked cars and drivers who were reluctant to let her out. Abruptly, she jerked off one of her shoes.

She attacked the plate glass window in front of them with a sharply spiked heel. She hit it again and again. The heel split.

But the window remained completely intact.

The glass was thick, tough; reinforced. They were prisoners in a car speeding north towards the wild Baluba area.

Angela said: 'Trois can't know anything about this.'

Wallace felt like kicking himself for not telling Brand about this trip. He didn't even have a gun. His carelessness looked like ending in a big story for the *Morning Post . . . Famous Columnist hacked to Death!* He could imagine the headline now . . .

The black Armstrong Siddeley limousine flashed through a native village, scattering squawking hens. Cliff Wallace and Angela De Villiers beat on the car windows with their hands to attract attention. Dark, impassive faces briefly caught their performance — and ignored them.

The car roared on, through wild desolation, taking them — where, and to what savage fate?

Wallace's face was solemn. 'Looks like we're for it, Angela honey. Looks like we're really for it!' he said.

Brand fed power to the green Studebaker convertible. He was through the suburbs of Elizabethville, racing north along the broad smooth highway. He saw no sign of the black Armstrong Siddeley.

His face was lean, savagely determined. His lips were set in a thin, taut line; his blue-grey eyes held a cold and bleak light. He thrust his foot down hard on the accelerator. He wanted the man M'Polo, and he wanted him alive — to force him to talk. Nor was this the only reason for Brand's breakneck speed.

Wallace and Angela De Villiers were in deadly danger. He didn't doubt it. He had to catch that Armstrong Siddetey before anything happened to them.

Then he saw a United Nations roadblock dead ahead.

Simultaneously, he saw something else: a rapidly moving dust cloud on his right.

Brand put two and two together with lightning speed, and thereafter prayed that he wasn't mistaken. He didn't pause; didn't hesitate. He went off the road. He went after the dust cloud. He didn't think that M'Polo would have chanced a brush with the U.N. and run the serious risk of being turned back. He was as sure as he could be of anything that the reddish cloud marked his quarry.

The Studebaker rattled as it jolted over bumps and holes in the loose dirt track; gravel rattled like hail against the bodywork. Brand drove at a recklessly high speed over the crude surface, swaying at the wheel as the car rocked from side to side. He had to keep that dust cloud in sight . . .

He flung the Studebaker forward between wild stunted brush under the blue dome of the sky. The sun climbed, a burnished copper disc. All about him was an eroded landscape, desolate, with an air of brooding menace. There was no sign of habitation.

Somewhere ahead, M'Polo raced the black limousine . . .

Foot hard down on the accelerator, Brand swung the wheel as the rough track twisted and turned. The car leapt and bucked. The springs protested at the treatment they were receiving.

Brand used every trick of driving technique that he knew to get the maximum speed from the Studebaker. The miles fled past, jagged flints beating a tattoo under the mudguards. A puncture now could mean disaster, but Brand did not let up for one moment. Two lives might well depend on his catching M'Polo before the big driver reached his intended destination.

And then Brand suddenly realized there was no longer any dust cloud to follow.

He swore; braked to a skidding stop, and climbed out from behind the wheel. He walked forward, studying the road surface. There were no fresh tyre-tracks in the red dust. No vehicle had passed this way in the last few days.

Brand straightened up. He stared bleakly round at barren wasteland and sun-baked, stunted brush, and his heart sank. He saw no sign of life anywhere.

He had lost the trail.

★　★　★

Wallace sat hunched up in the back of the black Armstrong Siddeley as it plunged headlong across undulating bushland, its tyres screaming in protest, its exhaust-pipe rattling. It was hard for Wallace to think clearly with every bone in his body taking a beating from the rough ride, but he was thinking — desperately.

He couldn't make up his mind. Would it be better to put up a fight as soon as the car door was unlocked — or wait it out, hoping for a break later? Perhaps the very best they could hope for was a quick death . . .

He tried not to remember the atrocity stories he'd heard — and had himself written up — of death by slow mutilation, organs and limbs being hacked off one after the other . . .

He gripped Angela's hand tightly. They had no words to say to each other now. There was no longer anything left that could be said.

Then the car slackened its furious pace and swung off the track. Tufts of grass showed momentarily; then they bumped down a slope. They had arrived at the end of their journey.

Before them lay an abandoned copper mine, a vast gaping hole in the landscape — a rust-red scar, with blue hills far off in the distance. Stepped clay banks descended in a series of levels. There were tumbledown wooden shacks and a cannibalised power shovel sprawled on its side like a great mechanical beetle.

The car stopped. Wallace took a deep breath, forced a wan smile. 'Well, this is it, baby . . . '

Africans seemed to spring up out of nowhere. They surrounded the car. There was a score or more of them, some naked except for a G-string, some in tattered remnants of *Force Publique* uniform, some wearing gaily-patterned calico shirts and khaki shorts. But all carried weapons, rifles, spears, pistols, bicycle chains, and all had something else in common, too. Hate-filled, malevolent eyes.

The blood ran cold in Wallace's veins. So much for his planning. He had no choice. No choice at all. The car was surrounded, and there were just too many of them for him to have any kind of chance.

Beside him, Angela De Villiers shuddered. She tugged at his arm, pointing, mute. Then Wallace saw what she'd seen already.

He saw severed white hands dangling from the belts of the Africans surrounding the car. He had no hope at all now. They had travelled very far north indeed . . . these men were invading Balubas!

M'Polo unlocked the car door, and wrenched it open. His head jerked: 'Out — you white monkeys!'

Strong brown hands reached inside and grabbed Wallace. He was dragged bodily out of the limousine. He struggled to remain on his feet and tried to keep a grip on himself, to submerge the feeling of abject despair that welled up within him.

M'Polo spat in his face. He took off his chauffeur's cap and slashed the hard peak across the bridge of the journalist's nose. Wallace staggered back, pain and blood blurring his vision. He heard Angela cry out.

Bracing his mountain of a body on broad, splay feet, M'Polo raised an arm the size of a ham. He balled a huge fist, and swung.

He hit Wallace once. Once was enough. Cliff Wallace went down — and out. Poleaxed.

And, as consciousness left him, Wallace heard Angela scream . . .

10

Dark Ritual

Simon Brand was sweating, worried sick about Angela De Villiers and Wallace. Already M'Polo had had time to do his worst with them — and he was no nearer to picking up their trail again.

He drove back along the dusty red-earth track that wandered across a scrub-covered wilderness. And, as he went, he asked himself savagely just how M'Polo had eluded him. Somewhere, there must be a turn-off. He drove more slowly now, watching sharp-eyed for tell-tale tyre-marks. When he found the Armstrong Siddeley tracks he would follow . . . but by then he might be too late.

Nevertheless, he forced himself to drive slowly and very carefully. He could not afford to miss the turn-off a second time.

There was a bend in the road, an

outcrop of rock. He swung the wheel of the Studebaker, and pulled up dead.

A Land Rover was parked across the track, blocking it. And guns covered him.

The faces behind the guns were hard and cold. There were the faces of white men who wore Katangese gendarmerie battledress.

No doubt these were the much-discussed, often-denigrated 'mercenaries' of Tshombe's army, Brand thought. He climbed from the Studebaker and walked towards them, keeping his empty hands well clear of his body and the gun holstered there. It might be they were trigger-happy.

The man in command of the white soldiers jumped down from the Land Rover before Brand reached it. He was a short man, stocky. He had straw-coloured hair and a skin burnt brick-red by the sun. He had ice-blue Nordic eyes, and he looked tough. His body was heavily muscled. He carried an automatic weapon with a knowledgeable air.

Brand said urgently, 'I'm employed by Cornelius Van Cleve and I need your help. I'm looking for a black man called M'Polo. I believe him to have kidnapped two journalists and brought them into the bush. I lost the trail somewhere around here.'

Blue eyes regarded him warily. 'I'm sorry, but we're paid to fight, not to wet-nurse reporters who stick their stupid necks out! Anyway, they don't give us much of a write-up. They don't put the truth about us in their dispatches to their newspapers. Serve 'em right!'

One of them is a woman,' Brand said swiftly. 'A white woman.'

'That's different. Why didn't you say so straight away? Let's get after them, Sam!' The speaker was another of the armed men, still aboard the Land Rover.

Their commander turned, frowning. 'Let's see what we're getting into first,' he said shortly. He faced Brand again, and there was calculation in his cold, ice-blue eyes. 'Van Cleve, eh . . . ?' Then it seemed as though something clicked inside his mind. He said quickly, 'Your name wouldn't be Brand, would it?'

'Yes,' Simon Brand said. 'I only arrived

in Elizabethville yesterday, and my job is top secret. But Mr. Van Cleve will vouch for me — '

But there the other man interrupted, and his wary expression had now completely gone. 'No need,' he said. And he was smiling. 'I've heard of you, Mr. Brand.' He thrust out his hand. He had a hard, powerful grip, Brand discovered. 'My name's Wesley. Sam Wesley.'

A slight pause emphasised the name, and he seemed to wait as if expecting Brand to recognise it. But the detective didn't. Sam Wesley . . . ? No one had mentioned a man of that name to him.

Now Wesley went on, 'The old mine's the most likely place to hold prisoners hereabouts, Mr. Brand. We've been watching it, off and on, for a couple of days now. There's something odd going on there.'

'Lead the way,' Brand said crisply. 'And I need M'Polo taken alive. He has some important questions to answer.'

Sam Wesley nodded. 'Fair enough. We'll do what we can. But I'm not prepared to risk the lives of my men unnecessarily. Mr. Brand.'

He swung away, towards the Land Rover.

'All right, boys, let's get moving! We might be in time to save what's left of 'em.'

A wave of his arm, and the Land Rover shot forward. Wesley swung himself effortlessly aboard as it came abreast of him. Brand followed in the green Studebaker. The two cars crashed their way through scrawny vegetation, rattled over loose jagged flints, and finally came to the crest of a great, circular shallow depression. It was a massive, brick-red scar scooped out of the earth by power shovels long before: the site of the old mine that the man called Sam Wesley had spoken of.

And now Brand heard the muted sinister beating of drums above the roar of the car's engines, and knew that Wesley had led him to the right place.

But had they arrived in time?

As the Land Rover screeched to a stop, Brand leapt from his own car, pulling out his Luger. The next instant, as if snapped off by the flick of a switch, the drums ceased to beat and a thick blanket of unnatural, ominous silence fell over everything. But it was a silence that did not last long.

The next moment it was carved in two by the sound of a woman screaming in abject terror.

Then Brand ran.

His face pantherish, his heavy Luger raised and ready to fire, he ran flat out towards the source of that terrible cry.

But in his heart, he felt he was too late . . .

★　★　★

When Cliff Wallace struggled back to consciousness he felt as if someone had been using his head for a football. He had difficulty in breathing. One eye was filmed over. He shook his head . . . and groaned as sudden pain stabbed through his skull.

He tried to move, and he couldn't. Needle-sharp spikes tore his flesh. A slow trickle of blood from his arms and legs made him itch maddeningly. He stared blearily down. He was tied hand and foot with barbed wire. Wire that had been drawn so cruelly tight that the barbs dug into him.

'Cliff!' An urgent feminine voice penetrated his aching brain. 'Cliff, are you all right?'

He turned his head a fraction, cautiously. Near him, also tied up, lay Angela De Villiers. There were dark weals across her cheek.

'Angela . . . ' Wallace muttered. 'What goes on?'

'They're saving us — for later. They're not quite ready for us.' Her voice was dull. 'Not quite ready . . . '

Wallace said, 'Hold on, honey, we're not dead yet.' And he glanced quickly around.

He saw huge steps cut into a red clay wall. He saw black bodies glistening with sweat as Baluba tribesmen danced under the copper sun to insidious pounding drums. Black feet stamped the red earth savagely, throwing up clinging dust.

Other men drank avidly from Coca-Cola bottles.

'Hell,' he croaked, attempting to summon up a smile, 'it's just like Notting Hill Gate on a Saturday night. I could use a drink myself.'

Angela darted a swift, apprehensive look at him. 'Not that kind, Cliff,' she said. 'They open the bottle and put raw rice into the Cola — then seal the bottles, again. They leave them lying around in the sun, and the mixture ferments very quickly. The result makes red biddy taste like lemonade. It's horribly potent.'

Wallace studied the drinkers again. Their bodies swayed and their eyes were glazed over.

'I see what you mean,' he said grimly.

Then M'Polo stalked over the ground. He kicked Wallace in the kidneys again and again. Wallace gagged on his agony and rolled with the boot, barbed wire tearing his flesh. He left a trail of blood, dark against the red earth.

'You are going to die, Mister Newspaperman,' the big Baluba declared thickly, and paused. Then he added, 'Slowly . . .'

He rolled unsteadily on his big splay feet.

'But the woman . . . ' he said, 'she won't die — yet.' He leered in Angela's direction. 'Though before we're through with her she'll be praying for us to finish her off!'

Wallace cursed the man, bitterly. 'You won't get away with this! There'll be a search for us. And when Tshombe's soldiers catch up with you, you big ape, they'll hang you!'

M'Polo's eyes glittered. 'You won't be around to see it. You start to die now!'

He grabbed up a knife. A knife with a long savage blade and a razor-sharp point stained black at the tip. The other Balubas gathered round swiftly. The time had come to watch this white man die.

Cliff Wallace shuddered. Why don't I keep my big mouth shut, he thought fatalistically. And he watched the knife, fascinated. It was to be all his, every glittering inch of it.

The Baluba called M'Polo said, 'You think you are clever, you people, but you are not so clever as our witch doctors.

They mix the poison from the liver of crocodiles with the venom of snakes. The result will destroy a man's nerves, paralyse his heart, and dissolve the blood in his veins. This is going to happen to you. You will be dead inside sixty seconds . . . but for you, that minute will seem like an endless eternity. An eternity of unendurable, screaming agony!'

He held the knife against Wallace's throat, and Wallace stared down at it, dry-mouthed. So he was going to die — here in the wilderness — and Dixon would get his 'Around and About' column for good. Even in his last moments of life, that thought irked him. And Angela . . . he tried not to think what horrors were in store for her.

Then M'Polo said — 'Now!'

And he raised his arm to strike the death blow.

And the drums stopped.

That was when Angela De Villiers screamed again.

★ ★ ★

Brand was running hard. He passed the black Armstrong Siddeley limousine and stared down the stepped walls of the opencast mine. He saw a savage tableau.

Below him, ringed by Baluba tribesmen, Cliff Wallace lay bound with barbed wire and abjectly helpless. Over him towered a huge black man in chauffeur's uniform, a vicious-looking knife glittering in a raised hand, ready to strike.

A few yards from Wallace, Angela De Villiers was surrounded by half-naked natives and screaming . . .

Brand knew he had to act fast. But even as he threw up his Luger and squeezed off a shot he aimed to disable rather than kill. He wanted the man M'Polo alive to answer some vital questions.

M'Polo was a key to the urgent problem of how to save President Tshombe from assassination, and the whole of Katanga from the imminent threat of rapine and murder.

Simon Brand fired.

His single shot echoed round the clay walls. Echoed and re-echoed again. The long, wicked knife was punched clean out of M'Polo's hand, and the big Baluba wheeled around unsteadily, a sick expression forming on his glistening dark face.

Brand went leaping down the giant steps cut in the crumbling red earth, his Luger held ready for further action. Behind him, automatic weapons stuttered savagely as the white Katanga mercenaries scattered the rest of the Balubas. One or two of the tribesmen dropped, writhing. The others sprinted for cover.

Brand shouted sharply above the noise: 'Don't move, M'Polo — or you're a dead man!'

The Baluba hesitated, poised for instant flight.

He saw the gun in Brand's hand and seemed to realise that it was a bullet from this weapon that had disarmed him. He froze. It was as if he suddenly appreciated that he'd just been given a demonstration of how accurate and lethal Brand could be with a Luger. One such demonstration was plainly enough.

Brand leapt down the rest of the giant steps gouged out of the red earth to reach him.

He was going to question this man ruthlessly just as soon as he'd ensured that Angela De Villiers and Wallace were safe. He was going to get some vital information out of M'Polo — so he thought. But he never did.

For, at that precise moment, the big Baluba moved. He shifted his weight from one splay foot to the other, and for someone above and behind Brand that was enough.

The sound of an automatic weapon sawed through the air. A stream of bullets leapt past Brand and hammered into M'Polo. They almost chewed the Baluba in half.

He was pitched backwards, the impact of the bullets, which still ploughed into him, making him spin on his toes like a grotesque ballet dancer. He fell on one side with his bloodied entrails spilled into the dust.

Brand ran to him and crouched down. But M'Polo had nothing to say, nothing at all. He wouldn't be talking ever again. He was dead.

Brand rose, breathing hard. He wheeled around and came face to face with Sam Wesley, who held a smoking Belgian-made sub-machinegun. Ice-blue Nordic eyes regarded Brand worriedly. 'Sorry, old man. I'm afraid I overdid it a little.'

Brand was very angry. 'I told you I wanted him taken alive.'

Sam Wesley shrugged apologetically.

'Sorry, old man,' he said again, and his voice was coloured with real regret. 'But I thought he had another trick up his sleeve, and I guess my enthusiasm and my gun lust ran away with me.'

Brand knelt in the dust beside Cliff Wallace and began to unwind the wire binding his friend. He worked carefully. Some of the barbs were deeply embedded.

'You'll never know how glad I am to see you,' Wallace said gratefully. 'But how — ?'

Brand didn't have to worry about the beautiful Angela De Villiers. She was the centre of attraction. Half a dozen of

Tshombe's European soldiers were engaged in releasing her — and enjoying every moment of the experience.

Brand helped Wallace to his feet. 'How d'you feel, Cliff?' he asked sympathetically. 'Think you can make it to the top?'

Cliff Wallace, battered and blood-stained, lit a cigarette with a shaking hand. His crumpled face cracked in a rueful grin. 'I can make it to the nearest bar . . . and a phone! I've got a good story! Personal angles stuff!'

Brand hid a smile. Once a newspaper-man, always a newspaperman!

He returned to the body of M'Polo and searched his pockets; he found nothing of use to him. But when he stood up again he was looking at the body of the Baluba in the chauffeur's uniform with a very thoughtful air — and he had his reasons.

Something had just clicked into place in Brand's mind.

11

United Nations—Go Home!

Voices howled frenziedly in the streets of Elizabethville. A tumult of sound filled the air — an angry, ominous sound.

The tumult reverberated between tall office blocks and neat brick dwelling houses. It rose to a roar, which had harsh undertones of definite menace. And then it was suddenly channelled into a chant that grew louder and louder as more and more voices took it up all the way across the city.

'*L'oni, au re-voir! L'oni, au re-voir!*'

Windows rattled.

Over and over again the chant echoed, accompanied by naked feet stamping out the staccato syllables. Pots and pans, and anything else that came to hand and made a noise, clanged out the beat.

'*L'oni, au re-voir! L'oni, au re-voir!*'

'L'oni, au revoir. United Nations — go home!'

Traffic stopped. A mob of Katangese rampaged through the broad avenues and shaded arcades of Elizabethville, vengefully bent on attacking anything or anyone associated with the detested United Nations.

Amid showering glass and rending metal, cars were bounced over on to their backs — some still with United Nations' drivers and passengers inside them. Stones flew like hail, and the windows of the American consular bungalow were rudely shattered. Five Ethiopian United Nations soldiers were dragged away from an early afternoon visit to a house of ill-fame and savagely beaten up, and a young raven-haired secretary working for a member of one of the United Nations' civilian delegations was pulled from the car in which she was riding and very roughly manhandled before being released by the mob.

That raven-haired secretary was a young woman called Crystal.

She had left Declan O'Donovan's bungalow in the United Nations' encampment half an hour earlier, intending to go shopping. But she never did. When the mob had finished with her, she had one thought — to get back to the bungalow and be safe behind the barbed wire encircling the United Nations' encampment, with armed sentries between her and the rioting Katangese. All she wanted was to get back there — fast.

This was her first thought, and it was instinctive. Her body shivering and shaking with shock, she went back to the camp and Declan O'Donovan's bungalow at a lurching, near-hysterical run. Her primary concern was for her immediate security and safety.

But, inevitably, a little while later, other thoughts came . . .

*   *   *

Declan O'Donovan was tense.

He paced his small office like a caged beast — to and fro, back and forth — his feet fraying the carpet.

He was waiting for somebody, and he was on edge. He was expecting an important visitor.

He heard the distant growl of angry noise from the city beyond the barbed wire entanglements marking the perimeter of the U.N. camp, but it didn't register with him. He was far too preoccupied with thoughts of his own past, and — more important — his future.

Declan O'Donovan's immediate past had been precarious.

A second-class degree in the humanities from a third-class university had earned him no kind of a living at all in his native hometown, nor in Ireland at large, nor in England. Hoping for better things he had gone to America.

But there he had found that, if anything, the competition for jobs was, in fact, keener. He had nearly starved. But then he had gravitated to New York and to the company of liberal Americans of all ages, sexes, and colours, and he had lived on his professedly left-wing beliefs and his Irish charm.

Particularly his native charm. It hadn't gone down well in Ireland — but it worked well enough in America.

Even so, for more than a year he hadn't known which ill-favoured but love-hungry middle-aged woman his next meal was coming from.

Then, completely by chance, he had met Crystal. And, straightway, life had taken a turn for the better. She had got money for him and, as a result of her earnest endeavours he had managed to swing his present job with the United Nations. But he had no illusions.

He knew that in another year — two at the most — his present job would come to an end, and then where would he be? There was only one answer. He'd be out in the cold. He wasn't a gifted administrator, or negotiator, or anything else. When his contract came to an end it would not be renewed. His own fellow-countrymen, he had discovered, had little use for him.

So he'd be out in the cold, and having to start all over again from scratch. Crystal — his key to jobs that his own doubtful ability certainly couldn't obtain for him — would be just that much older, and looking it. In any case, she would be more difficult to handle.

There was only one conclusion any man could reach, facing up to these facts, and Declan O'Donovan had long ago not only reached it but acted upon it. If he did nothing, just worked at his job, his future would be every bit as precarious as the immediate past. So he had to exploit his present position, make use of it in any way that he could, legal or illegal, moral or otherwise. He couldn't afford to be choosey.

Nor had he been.

The important visitor he was expecting was a man who could contemplate bloodshed and violence and murder with complete equanimity. And he was a man with a monstrous criminal plan.

Declan O'Donovan was going to help him put that plan into effect. It was all arranged. O'Donovan was going to exploit his present position with the United Nations for personal profit. He was all set to guarantee for himself a rosy future.

But still he was tense — waiting. He

paced his office, this way and that. He'd be glad when the job was done.

The truth was he'd been jumpy ever since Simon Brand had arrived in Elizabethville.

O'Donovan heard scurrying footsteps stumbling over themselves to reach the bungalow.

He stopped pacing his office abruptly. He frowned.

The footsteps lurched up on to the perch at the other end of the building where the living quarters were situated. Woman's footsteps. Distraught footsteps. Crystal's — ?

Declan O'Donovan heard a door jar inwards at the other end of the building. He started to move towards the sound.

Then he stopped. Another sound stopped him. The sound of the outer door of his office opening behind him.

He wheeled around. His important, expected visitor had arrived.

What happened then was that Crystal, still half-hysterical after the rough treatment she had received at the hands of the mob, came in search of sympathy, and comfort, and a shoulder to cry on. But she didn't find any one of these things.

She tried to open the communicating door between living quarters and office, and Declan O'Donovan blocked the door's arc of travel. He let the door open only so far, a few inches. He saw Crystal and, at the same time, didn't see her. He didn't take in any detail.

O'Donovan had been on edge all afternoon, and now his long-awaited important visitor had arrived and was actually in the small office with him. He had no time to spare for Crystal; not at this moment. He was obsessed by the knowledge that, now his important visitor had arrived, the next twenty minutes or so might well determine the shape of his whole personal future.

Crystal pushed at the door.

'Later!' Declan O'Donovan mouthed at her, fiercely impatient, and very conscious of the important man standing behind him. 'I'm busy!'

And he closed the door in Crystal's face, and he locked it.

If there was ever going to be a time for

Crystal to have serious second thoughts about what she was doing and where she was actually going, that time was now.

Crystal backed away from the locked door — fuming, almost white with anger. Then. Turning, she saw a glass and a gin bottle.

Bitterly, she slopped gin into the glass, added tonic water, gulped it down. But the spirit didn't do anything to drown her anger; nor did it shut off the drumbeat roar that came again and again from the distant city.

'L'Oni, au re-voir! L'Oni au-revoir! United Nations — go home!'

There was going to be serious trouble here, Crystal thought. It had already begun, and already she'd had more than her share of it. She slopped more gin into her glass; swallowed. She stared down at her torn and bedraggled dress.

Then a bitter surge of animosity towards Declan O'Donovan possessed her. It almost choked her. Tears of anger stood in her eyes. The swine — to treat her so cavalierly after all that she'd done for him! Who in hell did he think that he was? She'd show him! She'd just walk out on him!

And suddenly, hearing the voices of retribution in Elizabethville beating out and bellowing out their war cry again and again, Crystal decided to take their advice.

It was not only time to walk out on Declan O'Donovan, it was high time to get out of Katanga, too — while she still had a whole skin. Crystal's beautiful, creamy-white skin was precious to her. It was time to move on again. But where could she go to . . . ? And how would she get there? She had never bothered to save money. Always there had been another man ready and waiting to look after her. She sneered at that thought. Who, in fact, had been 'looking after' whom? She'd earned her daily bread in one way or another. But what to do now? How to get out of this place?

Then she heard muffled voices sounding through the partition between the living room and O'Donovan's office. So Declan had a visitor. Was that why he'd wanted her out of the way? Another woman?

Crystal crossed silently to the door and pressed an ear close to a panel. O'Donovan's voice came through clearly, high and shrill. 'Of course, I'm ready. Everything's prepared. You've only got to say the word.'

Then another voice reached Crystal. A man's voice speaking in a lower key. She had to strain to hear it. 'You've been careless, O'Donovan, Brand's partner is watching you like a hawk. I had to give him the slip to get in here.' The voice of the unknown man was flat, deadly, menacing. 'If you've let any part of this thing leak out — '

'He knows nothing!' O'Donovan protested. 'Shur, how could he?'

In the pause which followed, Crystal heard a rustle of paper.

'If anything goes wrong' — the flat voice sounded again — 'you'll get something you won't like, my dear O'Donovan. Something extremely unpleasant. We have ways of taking care of people who talk too much!'

'Nothing can go wrong!' O'Donovan's voice was eager now. 'I've got the letter here — see? All ready. Shur no one knows anything about it except myself.'

'What about that girl?' the other man intervened sharply. 'The one who tried to get in here.'

'Och,' O'Donovan said disparagingly, 'you've nothing to worry about with that one. Crystal wouldn't know what day of the week it was unless some man told her. And right now I'm the man. You follow me? I have my ways of making her do what I tell her, she's no threat to us. In any case, she knows nothing at all of what we're doing here.'

On the other side of the door, Crystal's expression hardened vindictively.

'All right . . . all right, Mister O'Donovan', she heard the other man in the office say. 'All right . . . but I'm just warning you. You're not indispensable.'

There was another pause. Then —

'You'd better get that letter off now. Right away. Things are coming to the boil here . . .'

'Yes, yes. I'll do that!' O'Donovan said.

Crystal heard the sound of a door opening and closing again. She darted to the window, hoping to catch a glimpse of O'Donovan's visitor. She hadn't recognised his voice. But she was unlucky, for the mystery man had slipped away unseen.

Crystal hesitated by the window for a moment, but only a moment, then she wheeled around. She knew what she was going to do.

Quickly, she crossed to the bedroom. Equally quietly, she changed her dress, and packed a bag.

Then, quietly, she slipped out of the bungalow. Brand's young partner was watching this place like a hawk, was he? Good! She looked around for him. After all, she felt, Nick Chandler owed her something. She had gone out of her way to be pleasant to Brand's young associate. Now, perhaps, he could help her.

He — or Simon Brand — would stake her to her fare home; she was sure of it. And, after that, once she was back in London and back in the swim, she'd be all right. But she had to find Nick and fix it all up.

He did owe her a favour — and Crystal's favours were worth something. And now, moreover, she had a tit-bit of news to bargain with. But where on earth was he?

Peering this way and that, she almost walked smack into the arms of the young man she was looking for.

She found Nick Chandler blocking her path, a hard and uncompromising expression on his face as he waited for her. She smiled brightly, 'Nick, darling!' Her butterfly lashes worked overtime. 'Just the man I wanted to see . . .'

Nick Chandler looked at her suspiciously. His gaze flickered over her attractive ensemble. She wore a travelling coat and carried a suitcase. He gripped her arm tightly. 'Where's O'Donovan?' he said.

Crystal kept smiling even though his grip hurt her arm. 'Declan's still in the bungalow,' she told him breathlessly. 'He won't be leaving. He's got an important job to do. The man said —'

'What man?' Chandler demanded.

Crystal contrived to look innocent — it wasn't easy. So Nick had missed O'Donovan's visitor. That made her news worth real money. 'Let's go somewhere we can talk, darling,' she suggested.

Nick frowned. He didn't trust her and he had no intention of being lured away from O'Donovan. 'We can talk right here,' he said.

Crystal arched an eyebrow coquettishly, then sighed almost instantly and let her expression sag. The hard, uncompromising look in Nick's eyes told her she was wasting her time. So she let the baby-mask fall away. What was the use of pretending?

Now she was her true self, the demure young miss was banished. Violet eyes revealed calculation; her mouth set hard. Suddenly, Crystal looked older.

'Declan had a visitor a few minutes ago,' she said. 'A man. He dodged you somehow . . . so that makes my story worth more. He gave Declan some instructions. You'll want to know what they were.'

Her manner convinced Nick now. Her sudden change of character was too abrupt to be anything but genuine. 'I'm getting out,' Crystal said levelly. 'Right out of Katanga. Out of Africa. And I'm going alone. I'm leaving Declan. All I want is my fare to England.'

'It's a deal,' Nick said quickly. 'Now tell me . . .'

*   *   *

The body lay on a cold slab in the police mortuary in Elizabethville. It was the body of a black man. Brand had gone to the mortuary immediately on his return to the city, and now he stared down with brooding intensity at the corpse on the slab.

It had shrunk in death, of course. But, in life, this man had never been tall. His body had been thin; now the loose skin hung in folds. It was not a pleasant sight, and when Brand had seen what he had come here to see he turned away.

The light in the mortuary was a harsh electric-blue. It splashed over bare stone walls and the stolid face of the senior police officer called Glaubeck. Brand said, 'This was Stephan Trois' real chauffeur?'

He'd already got Angela De Villiers' story of how Stephan Trois had promised to provide a car and a driver for her trip to the fighting in the north . . .

Glaubeck scratched his thick-featured face with a broad fingernail. '*Oui!*' he said, grunting. 'M'sieu Trois found the body himself, and reported the fact to me in person immediately. Presumably this man was murdered by M'Polo, who took his place . . . '

Simon Brand nodded.

'M'sieu Trois was mostly concerned for the safety of Mam'selle De Villiers and her escort,' the big Belgian went on. 'He'll be very relieved to hear that thanks to your own prompt action they haven't come to any real harm. Indeed, the only people who seem to have suffered in this affair are this poor devil here — ' the big policeman nodded towards the corpse on the slab, ' — M'Polo, who deserved all he got, and M'sieu Trois himself . . . '

'Trois . . . ?' One of Brand's eyebrows lifted. 'How so?'

'He's lost a good chauffeur, and possibly had his limousine damaged,' Captain Glaubeck said seriously. Obviously, it was a matter of some consequence if Stephan Trois' car had been harmed. It seemed to Brand that Stephan Trois must be regarded as a Very Important Person in Elizabethville.

He said shortly, 'A Captain Wesley of the Katanga Army was arranging to have the car driven back here.'

'Good,' Glaubeck said, nodding. Then — 'And that is all you required, *m'sieu?* To see the body of this poor, misfortunate man?'

'That's all,' Brand's tone was positive. A vague suspicion at the back of his mind assumed definite shape. He had come here to compare the proportions of M'Polo and the dead man on the slab, and this was just what he'd done.

He left the mortuary then. It was time to talk to Cornelius Van Cleve again. Events were marching fast to a climax.

Almost two days had gone by since

he'd accepted Van Cleve's commission. Little more than twenty-four hours remained in which to save the president of Katanga from certain assassination. Could he do it? He had to! And he had to move quickly!

12

Shadows

'But you have made some progress, Mr. Brand?' Cornelius Van Cleve demanded impatiently. 'I thought you wanted to see me to report your findings. Instead — '

He gestured abruptly with an open hand.

Instead, Brand had been firing questions at him. He was still seeking information when what Cornelius Van Cleve wanted were results.

The two men faced each other across a wide desk in the Belgian's office, in the Union Miniere building. It was a spacious office, with Venetian blinds filtering out the glare of the sun.

Brand smiled and took a cigarette from his case and lit it. He blew a plume of smoke towards the ceiling. 'Yes,' he said confidently, 'I think I can claim to have made some progress. M'Polo is dead. He paid with his life for the murder of the young boy Nsambo — and the boy's mother.'

Van Cleve said: 'If I understood you correctly, you wanted M'Polo to talk. Yet now he is dead, and he did not talk. This is a step forward?'

'In a way ... ' Brand replied enigmatically. 'Believe me, Mr. Van Cleve, even a dead man can talk — if you know how to listen.'

'I don't understand you,' the Belgian said frowning.

'You will,' Brand told him, 'eventually. Now tell me how the Compagnie Internationale of the Katangese Army operates.'

'Those who are not Katanga-born,' Van Cleve said, 'are recruited in Johannesburg and in Bulawayo, in Southern Rhodesia. They are all men with good service records, used to stern discipline. The idea is that they will form an élite, a backbone to the native gendarmerie. They are well paid for their trouble ... between a hundred and a hundred and eighty pounds a month with an additional bonus of four pounds for every day spent in action. They are fully insured, and receive a monthly allowance, and a furlough after one year's service.

'There are, so far, five platoons of these men armed and equipped ... and the world calls them soldiers of fortune, or worse. But I assure you that a surprisingly high proportion of these men are idealists, despite what the world Press thinks. Many of them are fighting for something that they believe in.'

Brand stubbed out his cigarette. He said: 'But who are they directly responsible to? Who, other than President Tshombe himself, commands them? Who gives them their orders?'

Van Cleve told him.

★　★　★

After that, Simon Brand waited.

He returned to the Hotel Livingstone, showered, and ate a substantial meal. Then he lay in his shirt-sleeves on the bed in his room, smoking and waiting. Van Cleve had promised to locate Stephan

Trois. He waited for the call that would tell him where Trois was to be found and, despite his reassuring words to Van Cleve, Brand was a very worried man.

He knew the sands were running out for Moise Tshomba. Thoughts buzzed in his head. Stephan Trois . . . Doctor Yoruba . . . Where did Declan O'Donovan fit into the picture — if at all? And where had Nick got to? He should have reported by now . . .

He switched off his train of thought. He guessed he knew most of the answers, but he could not be sure. That was why he must see Stephan Trois — and Julius Yoruba — to be sure.

Wallace and Angela De Villiers had both sent off their stories. Now they were receiving belated treatment for their injuries. They were not seriously hurt, and Brand didn't expect either of them to remain more than a few hours in hospital.

Above the quiet purr of an electric fan, a sudden sound entered the room from the street outside the hotel. It was a heavy, rumbling noise. It was followed almost immediately by the roar of a crowd. Brand swung himself off the bed, crushing out his cigarette butt. He crossed quickly to the window, and stared out and down.

The United Nations had sent in armoured cars — an Indian division by the insignia on the armour plate. That they were here to stop trouble was no doubt the intention of the men at Lake Success . . . but Brand wondered if they might not cause more trouble than they stopped. The U.N. was not popular in Elizabethville. He heard knuckles rap on his door, wheeled about, and called out: 'Come in.' The neat black figure of an African houseboy stood in the doorway, holding a sealed envelope. Brand ripped it open.

It was not the message he had been expecting. His gaze raked the sheet of notepaper . . . this was from Nick, still squatting on Declan O'Donovan's tail. And it read

'*Crystal has flown out, London-bound. O'Donovan had a visitor, a man, but I missed him. Sorry. O'Donovan has just posted a bulky letter to the United*

Nations headquarters in Leopoldville.'

Brand scribbled a note to Nick, sealed it in an envelope, and handed it to the houseboy with a substantial tip. 'Take this reply to the man who gave you that letter for me.'

Then he settled down to wait again.

But he had not long to wait now before his call came.

*   *   *

One of Declan O'Donovan's hands was shaking. He couldn't stop it, try as he might, and thinking about it made it worse. The coffee cup clattered against his teeth, and he put it down hurriedly. Events, he told himself nervously, were mounting rapidly to some sort of climax.

The canteen in the United Nations camp had the gloomy, dismal air of a barrack hut. The serving counter was bare and moistly wet. The light was dim. There was a smell of disinfectant. It was not the sort of place in which Declan O'Donovan would normally have elected to spend an evening. But he felt he had no choice. He was waiting for the storm to burst.

He sat with his back to a wall, watching the door. On the small checkered table in front of him was his half empty cup of coffee. He'd eaten there — alone. *Alone!*

With Brand's young partner, Nick Chandler, at the next table, never taking his eyes off him, not for an instant. Staring at him all the time with steady concentration. Waiting for him to break.

He tried to forget Chandler's warning. It had been delivered only seconds after they'd both arrived in this place. Chandler had suddenly crossed to his table; stopped, and leaned forward. 'You are in danger, Mr. O'Donovan! You've been marked down for killing! Why don't you talk, and we'll find you a nice, safe prison cell to hide in . . . '

Still O'Donovan felt cold. And still he sweated. His soft hands were clammy with perspiration.

If things went wrong this time — and they had often gone wrong for Declan O'Donovan — he was finished. Really finished. If it became known what he'd done, he'd be ruined. And he certainly wouldn't be welcome back in Ireland!

But nothing was going to go wrong . . . he hoped.

He licked dry, reedy lips . . . and darted another nervous glance towards the door. He was badly frightened. This was why he hadn't dared leave the safety of the camp, even for the brightly-lit bar of the Hotel Livingstone. He would have to pass dark alleyways, and his nerve wasn't up to it.

Then, suddenly, he had a thought.

The idea of going to the Hotel Livingstone — seeking out the bright lights and, perhaps, a woman — was very attractive. Perhaps having a detective watching him might not be such a bad handicap after all . . .

But now anger stirred in him. If it hadn't been for Brand's young partner, Crystal would be still with him. Why had the little tramp left? He'd treated her right — hadn't he? He missed her. The bungalow was cold and empty without her.

Briefly, anger drowned out his fear, and he rose.

He moved for the door: a beanpole with sandy hair and pale eyes. He moved with the sinuous grace of a ballet dancer.

Automatically, Nick followed him.

Outside, past the dim glow of light from the canteen, black night pressed down on Elizabethville. Arc lights gleamed from the direction of the wire encircling the encampment, but O'Donovan moved away from them, and was swallowed up by deep shadows. He was heading for his bungalow.

He hurried along with tense, nervous steps. He had quite made up his mind.

He would go back to his bungalow and change, and then risk a trip into Elizabethville.

He hurried on across the U.N. encampment. Now he was deep in the shadows between two long, wooden, barrack buildings. And that was when a deeper shadow — the shadow of a man — detached itself from the surrounding gloom and stepped straight into his path.

Declan O'Donovan saw the sudden flash of a knife-blade.

He cried out — shrilly — as the blade buried itself deep in his stomach.

★　★　★

Nick Chandler left the canteen in O'Donovan's wake. The sudden dark after the light of the canteen, left him night-blind. For a moment, he lost sign of his quarry. Just for one brief moment.

Brand's message, delivered by the African boy, had been quite definite. 'Stay with O'Donovan — try to break him down, make him talk. His life is threatened . . . '

Then Nick heard a startled cry; a cry of alarm, somewhere ahead of him in the black night. He hurled himself forward; caught a glimpse of two men struggling. O'Donovan and another. He saw the sudden gleam of a vicious naked blade . . .

Nick cursed as he saw the United Nations official collapse with the hilt of the knife projecting from his chest. He grappled with a shadowy figure — a short, heavily-muscled man whose eyes glittered savagely. The man was tough, no amateur at the art of unarmed combat. He swung a hard punch, low down.

Nick, caught off-balance, tripped over O'Donovan's outstretched legs, and the killer struck him a brutal rabbit-punch. Nick swayed.

Then the flat of a hand, a rigid knife-edge with the full weight of a powerful body behind it, hit him across the Adam's apple. Tears blinded him. He gulped for air. And again he felt the force of a blow, driving him down.

Falling, he clutched an ankle; clutched it tenaciously; held on, weak with pain. A boot slammed against his ribcage and drove the air from his lungs.

Still he held on, numbed, his head singing. A flurry of rapid blows rained down on him, and his grip slackened . . . consciousness began to fade.

His adversary swore virulently.

A final savage blow on Nick's skull finished him. Just before he blacked out completely, he was aware of the sound of running feet . . .

★　★　★

'How are you feeling now?'

Nick swam up from a black pit. Harsh electric light hurt his eyes, and he winced.

He saw Brand crouched over him, a worried expression on his lean face.

Concern in his voice, Brand repeated: 'How are you feeling?'

Nick forced a rueful grin. 'I'll be okay, chief. Give me a minute — '

The pain eased and his eyes focused in the guardroom of the U.N. camp. He was sprawled in a big chair. O'Donovan's corpse lay stretched out on the floor at his feet. He saw that the knife had been removed. Now it lay in soft tissue on a trestle table.

He sat up, his head still swimming, 'The killer got away?'

Brand said grimly: 'Only just . . . he was lucky. The security men almost nabbed him.'

Nick struggled to collect his thoughts. He searched his memory for a description of the killer. Brand would want one. He said: 'He was a short man, well-muscled. There was something about his eyes — '

Brand cut in quickly: 'Don't worry about it, Nick — I can fill in the details.' He added to his young partner's description. 'Light-coloured hair, skin sunburned brick-red, cold blue eyes — very Nordic. You'll know him again. His name's Wesley. Captain Sam Wesley. He's one of the Katanga mercenaries.'

Nick blinked. 'How . . . '

'How did I know Wesley killed Declan O'Donovan? I've described the man you saw kill O'Donovan, haven't I?'

'Yes, but I don't understand how . . . '

Brand picked up the knife that Sam Wesley had used. 'I recognised this,' he explained. He held it very carefully, by the hilt. He said, 'It's the same knife M'Polo was going to use on Cliff. Wesley must have taken it after M'Polo was killed. And that black stuff you can see under the blood on the blade is poison — pure, fast-working poison. A native concoction, and deadly. You were lucky, Nick. If Wesley hadn't really rammed the knife home in O'Donovan you might have collected a slash when you jumped him. And even a scratch from the poisoned tip of this blade could be fatal!'

Nick felt his scalp rise. He gulped. 'Wesley must have really hated O'Donovan's guts!'

'I've no doubt he did,' Simon Brand said.

'He must have found out that O'Donovan was cooking up some murderous mischief against President Tshombe,' Nick said wonderingly. 'He found out, then — wham! Cripes, but these babies play rough! Though we seem to be on the same side, I can't say I like Wesley's methods very much.'

Brand gave him a long, searching look. 'You're sure you're all right now?'

'Of course I'm sure. Yes, chief. I'm fine.'

'Then there's something I want you to do,' Simon Brand said. 'I want you to find Wesley, and after you've found him, I want you to stay on his tail. I want to know where I can get hold of him if necessary — fast!'

13

Gathering Storm

Brand had got the address of Stephan Trois' private apartment from Cornelius Van Cleve.

He stood now, in the centre of Trois' living room, looking about him. All was neat and meticulous; there was a place for everything, and everything was in its place. Brand assimilated an atmosphere — the atmosphere of a room. The room of a man who was remarkably elusive and hard to find. A man of unknown origins, and of mystery and power. A man who, together with Dr. Julius Yoruba, exerted a considerable amount of influence in the local government.

Brand thought that Trois would be fussy in his habits; a man who appreciated comfort; a man of independent mind.

He roved around. The brandy was of an exclusive, highly expensive brand. The cheroots were cellophane-wrapped, each with a thin, beaten-gold band about its dark waist. Brand riffled through books in the glass-fronted bookcase. Trois, he decided, took his studies of the Congo very seriously indeed. He passed into the bedroom, and found white linen suits hung in orderly rows in a big wardrobe. Shirts and underwear were neatly stacked in drawers.

Brand worked slowly, checking over everything thoroughly. There were no private papers; nothing to give him the lead he had hoped he might find. Obviously, if Stephan Trois had any secrets he kept them in his head. He was a man distrustful of the written word.

Brand completed his search without interruption, and left, relocking the door after him.

He walked round the block to the garage. Trois' black Armstrong Siddeley limousine — returned, presumably, by Sam Wesley or one of the other mercenaries — was there, newly cleaned and repaired. Brand probed the dashboard lockers, and boot. Again he searched thoroughly, and again he found nothing.

He straightened up, thoughtfully.

He went back to Trois' apartment again and let himself in; silently; unobserved.

Then he seated himself in the big, comfortable armchair, facing the door. He took out his Luger, slipped off the safety-catch, and held the gun on his knee.

After that, he settled down to wait.

★   ★   ★

Nick was busy. He combed the bars of Elizabethville, moving purposefully from brightly-lit bistros to murky cellars where African jazz beat out through the long night. He walked warily along dark alleyways and bribed doorkeepers to let him into private clubs.

He kept moving; kept hunting Sam Wesley.

And everywhere he went he found an atmosphere of tension. It was reflected in black faces and white. A strange silence fell as he entered each and every new place; furtive eyes watched him. He felt the tension; the sense of expectation. Something violent and savage was due to break in Elizabethville before very long.

He continued his round of calls; viewed the local dancing girls with a critical eye; sampled the local brew. He asked questions. His was routine legwork, looking for one man amongst thousands. And, so far, he hadn't found a trace of him.

So now he moved away from the more modern parts of the city. He sought out the old. He went into the dimly-lit shanty-slum area of Elizabethville. A marketplace was silent; deserted. He walked in the shadow of mango trees, past rows of broken-down dwellings. He sometimes disturbed roosting hens.

And he came to bamboo walls vibrating with sound: the monotonous beat of drums and a rhythmic handclap. A native dancehall. He was very circumspect now, not wanting trouble. He looked in through an open window. There were black faces everywhere; no white men at all . . .

In the doorway, a young dark-skinned girl smiled at him. There was light behind her, revealing the silhouette of her lithe figure. A brightly patterned calico dress hugged her curves, one dusky shoulder bare. She called softly to him — an invitation. But Nick moved relentlessly on.

He imagined Wesley sleeping somewhere, in some hideaway. And he went on, his legs aching. Slowly, he worked his way round and back to the United Nations camp. He followed the wire.

There came a flicker of light in the darkness. Someone was guardedly using a flashlamp. Nick moved swiftly, He saw the ugly shapes of armoured cars drawn up in a row, machinegun barrels pointing at the black-velvet, star-dusted sky.

Someone was among the cars. An unauthorised someone . . .

Nick waited. The man left the row of cars and slid back through a break in the wire. He cat-footed away into the night — Nick following.

The man left the U.N. camp far behind.

Then, as he passed a café on the corner of a street near the city centre, the blood-red glow of a neon sign illuminated him briefly, and Nick saw him quite clearly.

He saw a short, stocky figure, heavily-muscled . . . fair hair and a skin burnt by the sun . . . Sam Wesley.

He shadowed him.

⋆ ⋆ ⋆

The room was in darkness. It was silent. Not a breath of air stirred in Stephan Trois' apartment. Simon Brand sat motionless in the deep armchair, Luger on his knee, waiting.

He was relaxed, but fully awake. He watched the door steadily, listening for the slightest sound from beyond.

The minutes ticked away.

Then came the faintest noise. A careful fumbling at the keyhole on the other side of the door. He tensed, lifted his Luger. There was a sudden, sharp click, and the door swung inwards. A shadowy figure hesitated in the opening.

A hand groped for a switch.

Brand was poised on a knife-edge of urgent expectation. The next second, the room was flooded with light.

Then Brand saw the person who had entered so stealthily. He saw her quite clearly. And she made a trim figure in safari shirt and bottle green shirt, with her broad silver belt.

She stood transfixed, staring petrified at Brand and the gun in his hand.

It was Angela De Villiers, the blonde from Johannesburg.

* * *

Angela De Villiers was startled. The Luger pointing directly at her stomach made sure of that. Then she recognised the man behind the gun, and forced a smile. Tentatively, she relaxed. 'Mr. Brand — you frightened me!'

Brand holstered his Luger slowly, and equally slowly rose to his feet. 'You were expecting to find someone else here, Miss De Villiers?' he suggested. Then, before she could answer, he went on smoothly,

'Stephan Trois is out of town . . . '

He saw from her expression that this was no news to her, but she hesitated to answer him. Why?

Then she slid a bent hairpin into her handbag, and her orange lips framed an uncertain smile. 'I — I wasn't expecting to find anyone here,' she told him. 'I'm a reporter — remember? I thought I might dig up some useful facts about Trois while he's away. That man fascinates me. There's a lot more to him than meets the eye.'

'And Cliff Wallace . . . ?' said Brand.

'I ditched him.' Her voice was cool and confident now. 'For a journalist, he's far too trusting . . . '

Brand thought that Wallace wouldn't be far behind her. The *Post* columnist wasn't that easily hoodwinked.

Angela De Villiers looked round the room. 'I suppose I'm wasting my time. Obviously, you've searched the place. No need to ask why you're here . . . waiting for Trois to return.'

For an instant, her teeth were bared. She looked angry. 'I really believe he wanted to get rid of me! I really believe he was responsible for trying to have me and Cliff killed! I'm rather interested in meeting Mister Trois again!'

She moved round the room on her thin high-heeled sandals. Brand watched without speaking. Her short skirt revealed very shapely legs. She ran a finger along the top of a bookcase, then helped herself to some of Trois' whisky. She inserted a cigarette into her long green holder. She seemed very much at home. Brand snapped his lighter for her, held out the flame. Now she was close, he could see flesh-coloured plaster on one cheek. And she was wearing a new shirt; the fabric was taut across her breasts, the cleavage deep. He caught a breath of delicate perfume.

'Well, Mr. Brand,' she said, drawing hard on her cigarette and looking at him expressionlessly through the smoke, 'what do we do next? Put out the light and wait . . . ?'

Her voice was almost a caress.

'I'm afraid that would be a waste of time — now. Your arrival here will have given the game away, Miss De Villiers. The people I'm out to nail are very clever — and careful.'

'Sorry!' Angela De Villiers grimaced. 'So I've spoiled things for you . . . well, maybe I could make it up to you.'

She was standing close to him, and looking at him in an odd way. But, just the same, he chose to misinterpret what she had said. He had been thinking.

So now he told her: 'It's quite possible that you can.' But his tone of voice was grim, unrelaxed, unrelenting, and made her look at him sharply. He said: 'You circulate a lot, Miss De Villiers. I think we can take that as read. And, particularly, as you're a journalist, you've got a trained eye, and a trained mind . . .'

'I suppose so,' the blonde agreed. But she was wary, wondering what was coming next.

'You get around a lot,' Brand reiterated. 'Especially in your native South Africa. You see a lot of places, and faces . . .'

There he paused, and she stared at him, eyes narrowing suddenly. Abruptly, she said: 'What are you? A magician? A devil? A mind-reader, or what?'

'Tell me,' said Brand.

Still staring at him, she said: 'I was going to mention it when I next saw you but . . . well, it just slipped my mind. The mercenary . . . you remember, the one who led the rescue party at the mine . . . ?'

'What about him?' said Brand, and his voice was flat now. Too flat. It was obviously held rigidly under control.

Angela De Villiers said slowly: 'He shot M'Polo . . . and I'm almost sure I recognised him. I've seen his picture somewhere . . . but I can't place him.'

Brand was nodding.

Angela De Villiers said: 'How on earth did you know?'

'I saw you look at him sharply — twice — down at the mine,' Brand said. 'He's a South African, too — or so he says. Actually, I doubt that. His name is Wesley, Sam Wesley. Does that ring any bells? I was hoping . . . '

Suddenly, Angela De Villiers stiffened.

'Now, wait a minute . . . ' she breathed. 'Wait a minute . . . '

But Brand's voice had hardened. 'I haven't the time!'

He said: 'A hell of a lot may hang on what you can tell me. So give it to me! Tell me what you've just remembered! President Tshombe's life is at stake here, and I'm not joking. Nor is that all! A reign of terror could be let loose in this country that would make what's been happening in the rest of the Congo look like a Sunday School toddlers' tiff!

'So tell me — ' Brand said ' — and tell me fast!'

14

The Killers

Preparations for the big Presidential rally had begun early. Since first light, crowds had been thronging the wide avenues, the shaded arcades and dim alleyways of Elizabethville. There was the raucous blare of a brass band, the beating of drums and the chanting of slogans: '*L'Oni, au re-voir! United Nations — go home!*'

Brightly coloured banners hung between the buildings; banners bearing defiant slogans. There was a general movement towards the flat grassland separating the United Nations camp from President Tshombe's palace. A large concourse gathered there.

The sun beat down brazen rays over a city gone wild. This was no carnival gaiety. The atmosphere was one of grim hostility to the provocative presence of United Nations' troops.

Word had gone round. The President was to address his people at noon. And there was little doubt in the minds of the Katangese about what he would say. He would denounce the U.N. He would call on them to withdraw their troops and leave Katanga in peace.

Some hotheads among the vast crowd anticipated their orders. They carried guns and machetes. They smashed windows. Already the main avenue of the city was a carpet of broken glass.

And isolated shots echoed from the direction of the U.N. camp.

No one was foolish enough to walk the streets wearing a U.N. armband that morning. The United Nations officials kept to their quarters and hoped for the best. They hoped the trouble would soon die down. But they were uneasy . . . Messages sped to Leopoldville, asking for fresh orders . . .

Outside, in the streets, the roar of the crowd grew in intensity. There was savage menace in the sound now, and a threat of riot. The Katangese gendarmerie was out in strength, supported by the white units of the Katanga army, but whether they were for or against the crowd yet remained to be demonstrated.

The U.N. commander, finding himself reaping the whirlwind sown by his woolly-headed superiors, could only do one thing. It was useless sending out foot soldiers, or even trucks, A handful of men could do nothing with a mob inflamed to retaliatory measures and ready for violence. But he had to do something; make some show of authority.

So he sent out his armoured cars to patrol the streets.

★ ★ ★

One of the armoured cars was soon in trouble. It developed an engine fault. It broke down near a covered arcade in front of shops closed and shuttered. It refused to go any farther.

The two-man crew — both Indians in khaki battledress — looked at each other inside the armoured car. It might be that only some slight adjustment was called for to get the vehicle moving again, but this would involve one or the other of them clambering out

And a crowd was gathering, pressing about the car, and beating on the sides of it angrily. The two U.N. men decided to stay where they were, safe behind thick armour-plate, and they radioed for assistance.

Help came — faster than they had expected. It came in the form of two white men in the uniform of the Katanga gendarmerie. One was short, with light-coloured hair and very blue eyes set in a face burnt brick-red by the sun. The other was tall, narrow-hipped and broad shouldered, with a broad-brimmed hat: a lean, laconic individual who answered to the name of 'Aussie'.

They came in a breakdown lorry. They hitched up to the armoured car and dragged it clear of the crowd. They towed it through deserted side streets and back alleys to an isolated garage.

Sam Wesley gave the thumbs-up sign to Aussie when they got there. Wesley was the other man in the breakdown truck, and everything had gone according to plan. He banged a fist on one of the thickly plated sides of the armoured car and called out: 'You can come out now — it's safe enough here.'

The two Indian soldiers emerged in a hurry. They wanted to get their engine working again. They felt naked outside their armour.

Wesley had already opened up the bonnet and was delving inside, doing something to the engine . . . He waved the Indian's back. 'You can leave it to me,' he said. 'I'm a good mechanic.' He gestured in the direction of the garage. 'Take 'em inside, Aussie. Fix 'em up with a cup of char. No telling how long this job will take.'

'C'mon,' Aussie grunted.

The two Indian soldiers hesitated.

They looked around anxiously; the angry sound of the mob was not very far off. It was only sensible to take cover and avoid provoking the civilian population any further. They had strict orders about that. They followed Aussie into the garage . . .

The fault didn't take Wesley long to

repair. He simply re-connected a fuel pipe he had slackened off the night before when he'd been out at the U.N. camp.

Suddenly there was a sound like a car backfiring, close at hand. Sam Wesley looked round, then bared his teeth in a cynical smile. 'Thirteen . . . ' he murmured, reading off the number painted on the side of the armoured car. 'Unlucky for some — and it's going to be even more unlucky for someone else shortly!'

He entered the garage. Aussie was there, covering something with a tarpaulin. There was blood on the oily, concrete floor.

Wesley said: 'Get behind the wheel of that armoured car, Aussie. And keep well down. I'll only be a couple of minutes.'

He went swiftly up a flight of wooden steps inside the garage.

Aussie went out to the armoured car.

*   *   *

Sam Wesley whistled between clenched teeth. There was a hard glitter in his ice-cold blue eyes. He was feeling good.

216

Everything was going exactly according to plan.

Armoured car Number Thirteen trundled slowly forward. It crawled through crowded streets, working its way towards the broad expanse of grassland between the Palace and the U.N. camp. It was here that the President was going to speak.

Wesley stood on the iron platform, his feet level with the driver's waist. He leaned against the barrel of a machine-gun, staring out through a narrow slit in the armour. He called directions: 'Left . . . straighten up, Aussie . . . straight ahead . . . steady . . . '

The driver, crouched low in his seat over the wheel, was a shadowy form. A cigarette dangled from his lower lip. The wide brim of his hat obscured his face. He grunted from time to time, driving expertly, carrying out Wesley's precise instructions.

They rolled out of the city along a wide avenue, and there before them was a vast sea of humanity — black and white citizens of Elizabethville — obscuring the green of the grass. The armoured car edged nearer, taking up a position behind the crowd.

Looking through his narrow slit, Sam Wesley saw a wooden platform, raised up in the centre of the concourse. It was fitted with a microphone and loud-speaker. He began to gauge distance, angles, wind velocity. He directed his driver to his final, chosen position. And then —

Wesley spoke to the driver crouched low in the well of the armoured car. 'Stop! No talking now, Aussie,' Wesley's voice was harsh. 'I need to concentrate, and I don't want any distractions. Just be ready to get the hell out of here when I give the word.'

The driver grunted a reply.

Sam Wesley picked up a rifle. It was a high velocity weapon fitted with a telescopic sight, and he handled it with loving care. It was his most cherished possession. No mother ever lavished more attention on her child than he on that rifle.

For Wesley was a professional. A professional killer. This was his calling.

This was his secret. He'd been round the world — and halfway round again — killing his way, making a good living.

And what he was about to do here — what he'd been hired to do here — would carry him up to new heights in his chosen profession.

For he intended to kill a man called Moise Tshombe. And never before had he been invited to liquidate a President.

15

Seconds to Zero

Sam Wesley glanced at his watch. It wanted only a few minutes to noon now.

The sun beat down, baking hot, on the thick steel plates of the armoured car. A fine sweat beaded his forehead. Yet he felt cool as the crowd cheered, and waves of hysterical noise beat about his ears.

He looked round steadily, checking up. The red-brick and concrete Palace was in the distance, high-walled and solid. The wire of the U.N. camp was at his back. No one seemed alarmed at the armoured car's appearance. It was just there, motionless, silent, waiting. All attention was focused forward, on the dais where president Tshombe would appear.

Sam Wesley waited, too — patiently.

He watched a car arrive, and saw it drive along a roped-off lane between ranks of hoarsely-cheering people. The noise of their shouted greeting stunned his ears, deafening him. He scowled, and forced himself to concentrate.

Now he saw a dark elegant figure mount the rostrum.

Slowly, cautiously, Wesley raised his iron hatch above his head. He glanced quickly round, and then eased the hatch fully open. Nobody saw him. All eyes were on President Tshombe. Wesley straightened up, head and shoulders clearing the hatchway.

He saw his target plainly, and licked dry lips. He carefully and cautiously raised his rifle and rested the barrel on the hatch coaming. He made himself comfortable. He took careful aim.

He thought ahead. It was lucky they had the car to get away in. Nothing would be able to stop them with Aussie driving hell-for-leather. And, if anyone tried, he'd use the car's machine-gun on them. It would be a piece of cake . . .

Words boomed from the loudspeakers. 'My people — '

Sam Wesley centred his weapon. The cross-wires were dead on target. He took

221

first pressure. And now . . .

Now nothing — nothing on earth — could save President Tshombe from certain death!

* * *

Simon Brand circulated among the dense-packed, wildly-cheering crowds on the grass plain, in front of the Presidential Palace.

His lean face was drawn. He looked — and felt — weary. His eyes were gritty from lack of real sleep throughout all the time he'd been in Katanga. But he drove himself relentlessly on.

His nerves were stretched as taut as a piano-wire as he looked quickly this way and that across the moiling, multi-coloured face of the crowd. After Angela De Villiers had told him as much as she could tell him about Sam Wesley, he had found out the rest of the facts for himself.

He had cabled Johannesburg — urgently. Angela had remembered seeing Wesley's photograph in a South African paper, but she had been vague about the exact context in which it had appeared. So Brand had set the cables humming.

And, just an hour ago, he had received a reply. A reply from the Chief of Police in Johannesburg. He had ripped open the envelope, and read:

WESLEY PROFESSIONAL ASSASSIN — STOP — WANTED HERE FOR MURDER — STOP — THIS MAN IS DANGEROUS.

★ ★ ★

So now Brand knew.

He knew that Sam Wesley, who had posed as a mercenary, was actually the assassin hired to kill President Tshombe.

And he knew something else deep in his bones: Wesley could be expected to make his murder bid at any moment. The planned assassination attempt was to be here and now.

Brand's face was grim as he patrolled the roped off aisle through which the presidential car must come. The all-important question pulsed and pulsed again through his brain. Where was

Wesley? Time was short. Time for President Tshombe of Katanga was fast running out . . .

The sun blasted down on Brand's neck. It was almost high noon. He guessed with dreadful certainty that he had only bare minutes left in which to find Wesley and stop him. At the back of the crowd he noticed an armoured car of the United Nations Indian division. The number painted on its steel hull was Thirteen. His gaze roved on, questing . . . but he noted the position of the armoured car in case he needed help later.

There was something else on Brand's mind, worrying him. Chandler had failed to report since he'd gone looking for Wesley the previous night. Brand knew his young partner to be tough and resourceful — and it was unlike him not to report back. It might be that circumstances had prevented that . . . or it might be something else again. Nick had taken quite a beating from O'Donovan's killer. And so Brand worried as he moved through the noisy, slogan-chanting crowd.

He heard President Tshombe's car approaching. He tensed for action. His intuition told him that only seconds were left now before the assassination attempt would be carried out. His blue-grey eyes desperately raked the sides of the lane for suspicious movement. Was there a bomb here . . . ?

Nothing happened.

The Presidential car reached the dais, and stopped. Brand waited, more tense than ever now, his eyes narrowed. *Where was Sam Wesley?* President Tshombe had mounted the steps of the platform, responding to the tumultuous acclaim with a beaming smile.

Then he stepped towards the microphone on the rostrum and now — suddenly — Brand saw movement. His eyes riveted on it.

Over the heads of the crowd, he saw the hatch of United Nations arnoured car Number Thirteen lift very slightly. He frowned. Then, in the next instant, the hatch was thrown completely back, and a man with fair hair and a face burnt brick-red by the sun . . .

Sam Wesley!

In that same split-second, Brand leapt into action. He recognised Wesley, and he moved instantly. And he moved fast.

He went for the armoured car, shouldering his way through the crowd, barging into people, thrusting them out of the way.

He was running.

Now he could see Wesley bringing up a rifle fitted with a telescopic sight. Now the assassin rested the rifle on the hard coaming, and took aim carefully.

Brand came out in a cold sweat. He redoubled his efforts to reach the armoured car. He had to stop Wesley! He had to reach the car in time!

He still had some distance to cover and he knew he couldn't break out his Luger. The crowd of Katangese, white and black, would easily misunderstand . . . and tear him to pieces.

He ran with set face, pounding the grass, shoving people out of his way. He sensed from Wesley's tense stance, that he'd already taken first pressure. In a matter of seconds, it would all be over,

President Tshombe would be dead.

Then Brand realised something. He had to admit it to himself, even as he continued to plough forward. He had failed.

He could not reach Wesley in time to stop him.

In another split-second, the murder shot would blast out — and then all hell would break loose. The people of Elizabethville would rise in their wrath. There would be a horrible bloodbath.

16

Death in the Sun

The hot African sun beat down the great concourse gathered before the Palace. It beat brazenly down on the lone figure clutching a microphone on the raised dais in their midst. And it turned the interior of armoured car Number Thirteen into an oven.

But Sam Wesley did not feel the heat of the sun. He stood, poised, savouring his moment of triumph. He held Tshombe's life in his hands! His rifle zeroed, his finger was taut on the trigger. He had planned for this moment, and now it had arrived. A tense moment. It was almost with reluctance that he made up his mind to shoot. In another second, Moise Tshombe would be dead . . .

And then something happened. Something completely unexpected. There was movement inside the armoured car. The driver crouched in his seat below Wesley's feet swung around and swung upwards. He lunged. He struck Wesley a paralysing blow in the solar plexus.

Sam Wesley collapsed. The rifle dropped from his hands with a clatter. Tears of pain blinding him, he gasped out, 'Aussie! What the — ?'

But the driver of the armoured car — the man with the broad-brimmed hat shielding his face — the man who had struck him — was not Aussie. Wesley could see that now.

The driver of the armoured car was Nick Chandler — Simon Brand's junior partner.

Wesley had no time to wonder what had happened to Aussie. Nick Chandler, remembering the beating that this man had given him, was in a savage and vengeful mood. He owed Wesley something, and now he settled the account and marked it 'Paid in Full'.

He slammed into Wesley with both fists, hitting hard and often with ramrod precision. Hitting where it hurt most.

Striving to put his man down and finish him fast.

But Sam Wesley was desperate. He knew that if he were taken his life would be forfeit. And he fought back savagely. Snarling, he lashed out with a steel-tipped boot . . .

Nick caught at his ankle, and twisted. Wesley fell heavily, swearing, his hard blue eyes ablaze with fury. Nick smashed down both his fists, together, into the killer's throat. He put every ounce of power he possessed into the blow.

Wesley made a choking, sobbing noise like a stricken animal. He writhed on the greasy floor of the armoured car. And Nick coolly put in the finishing punch. He knocked Wesley out cold.

That was when Brand arrived. Simon Brand had seen Wesley's head disappear down the hatch. Now he glared down into the car with levelled Luger, only to gasp —

'*Nick!*'

'Everything's under control, chief,' Nick said, panting. 'Thirteen was Wesley's unlucky number!'

Brand glanced back at the crowd. Tshombe was still speaking, holding their rapt attention. The struggle appeared to have gone almost unnoticed.

'Right!' he said briskly. 'Start up, Nick! We're taking this scoundrel straight to the police. He's going to sing and sing loud. He's going to prove my case against the men responsible.'

Nick slowly backed the armoured car away from the crowd. Very carefully, he reversed and drove into Elizabethville. And, as he drove, he told Brand the whole story . . .

'I picked up Wesley's tail all right, and he led me to a garage in the back-streets. There was another man waiting for him there. A character called Aussie. I didn't dare risk losing them to get to a phone. Obviously they were ready to move off, and I'd no idea what their plan was at that time.'

Brand lit two cigarettes, and passed one down to his partner.

'Thanks . . . well, I watched them pick up this armoured car. Then Aussie murdered the crew in the garage — I just didn't stand a chance of stopping that. Then Aussie came out of the garage alone.

'I clobbered him, put on this bush-shirt and this wide-brimmed hat of his, which covered most of my face, and got behind the wheel, hoping Wesley would lead me to the man who gave him his orders. But he didn't. Instead, he led me to where you found us. And all the time Wesley never realised that I'd changed places with this Aussie character, his pal.'

Nick took a long drag at his cigarette.

'As soon as we pulled in behind that crowd back there,' he said, 'I knew what the game was. But I didn't dare risk making a mess of things. I was well below Wesley, stuck down here, behind this wheel, and though that had saved me from recognition it was now something of a disadvantage. I just had to wait for exactly the right moment to clobber Wesley. His full concentration had to be somewhere else. If I'd chosen the wrong moment he would have just kicked my head in, and that would have been that.'

'You did a first-class job, old son.'

Brand said — and smiled ruefully. 'But I was certainly sweating during those last few minutes . . .'

His expression changed. Hardness entered his voice. His eyes held the chill of winter. 'But that's all behind us now, Nick,' he said. 'Now for the showdown!'

★　★　★

The Showdown!

This was also the thought in the brain of Doctor Julius Yoruba. It had come earlier than he had anticipated. It was here — now.

His handsome face twisted in a smile that was both cold and cruel. Everything had gone wrong. Moise Tshombe was still alive, still President of Katanga . . .

He stared bleakly at Stephan Trois. His voice rasped out, full of scorn. 'You fool! You bungled the job! Brand has got Sam Wesley, and Wesley will talk!' He trembled; the violence in him only barely held in check.

Across the room, Stephan Trois leaned

against the wall, one hand deep in the pocket of his cream-coloured lightweight jacket. A trickle of smoke rose from the thin black cheroot jutting from his mouth. He stroked his ginger spade beard, his eyes watchful and wary. He shrugged, almost imperceptibly. 'It was bad luck, Julius.'

Gold teeth glinted savagely. 'Bad luck . . . ?' Yoruba echoed. He almost snarled out the words. 'Brand will be here soon!' he said. 'You can rely on it. Simon Brand is coming here.'

Doctor Yoruba laughed. It was a harsh sound that hung in the air of the room. Thoughts raced through Yoruba's head even as he spoke.

He had no further use for Trois . . . *he* must be the scapegoat. Trois would take *all* the blame . . . it had been a mistake to rely on the cosmopolitan. His own people, the Baluba, would have served him better, but he was isolated here, in the south. Anyway, the mistake could be applied to a useful end. Doctor Julius Yoruba was not finished yet.

Faintly, far-off, the voice of the crowd

reached out and touched him. A frightening, blood-chilling chant carried on the air. It seemed to be coming nearer. 'What's that?' he demanded suspiciously.

Trois began to cough.

He coughed and coughed. He doubled up, gasping. He managed to get out: 'It's — it's the mob. Maybe they're going to attack the United Nations camp.'

Another paroxysm seized him. He thrust a hand flat against his heaving chest and thudding heart.

Quickly, Yoruba crossed the room to the cocktail cabinet. 'You need a drink, Stephan,' he said. 'Brandy?'

Trois had finally conquered his coughing fit. He nodded shakily. But then he suddenly seemed to wake up to what was happening, and he stiffened suspiciously. Yoruba's back blocked off all sight of the drink he was pouring.

Trois said carefully — a little too carefully — 'You'll join me, Julius, of course . . . ?'

'Yes . . . why not?' Yoruba said lightly. Too lightly? Trois regarded his broad back with the deepest suspicion.

For Trois also had no doubt that this was the showdown. And he had come prepared — prepared to sacrifice Yoruba. Brand's employer — Cornelius Van Cleve — wanted a scalp. Well, he'd get one . . .

He watched, narrow-eyed, as Yoruba turned with two brimming, ornate cut-glass tumblers, one in either hand. These the doctor carried carefully, delicately, across the room. He set them down on the table.

He pushed one tumbler across the mirror-polished surface towards Trois, and then picked up the other brimming glass carefully and sipped appreciatively. He smacked his lips. 'Wonderful stuff. But come, Stephan, you're not drinking with me . . . '

Trois stood motionless, his head tilted to one side, listening to the mob surging through the streets. Coming closer. He smiled thinly and crushed out the butt of his black cheroot. He waited for Yoruba to set down the glass from which he was sipping. He waited . . .

Then he reached out. But, at the last moment, his hand changed direction. It travelled to the glass from which Yoruba had already sipped.

'You wouldn't try to poison me, would you?' he gibed.

His hand fastened quickly on the tumbler.

And, as it did so, he felt the slightest prick from a rough-cut edge of glass. Instantly, paralysis gripped him. The tumbler fell from his numbed hand, and shattered. Brandy leapt across the leopard skin rug.

An angry pulse throbbed up his arm, his brain. It became agony to move. There was excruciating pain, like a white-hot fire consuming his body. He doubled up, screaming in agony. He vomited.

'Yes. M'sieu Trois . . . ' Doctor Yoruba's black face was shining. His gold teeth glittered. 'As you suspected — poison! But not quite in the way you imagined. The poison was on the outside of the glass . . . the roughed edge scratched your skin. That was enough!'

He looked down without pity at Trois writhing on the carpet. 'You have precisely eight more seconds to live!'

Trois' body arched. His face was grey, and tiny bubbles frothed at the corners of his twisted mouth. His eyeballs bulged from his head, and the room swung like a pendulum about him. He was dying — and Doctor Yoruba stood over him, laughing.

Trois ground out his last bitter words. 'Not . . . so . . . clever . . . as . . . you think . . . '

And then he died.

He died while the noise of the mob rampaging through the streets and arcades of Elizabethville grew ever louder. While the howling pack smashed its way ever nearer . . .

★ ★ ★

An angry roar filled the air. A swarm of men and women, black-skinned and brown, some with guns and machetes, others with broken bottles or cycle-chains, poured like a floodtide through the streets. Coming ever nearer . . .

Doctor Julius Yoruba was alone, looking down in silent contemplation at the body of Stephan Trois. It lay sprawled on his carpet, ugly in death.

Gradually, the noise outside penetrated his thoughts, and he frowned. Something had gone wrong again — something was always going wrong. The rabble should have been channelled away from his magnificent home. It didn't do to let the rioters loose in the most exclusive residential area in town. Damage might be done. Anywhere else, it didn't matter — but not here.

He started towards a telephone, to give orders to the police. Then he stopped. It was now too late for that. Already the mob was sweeping down the street, towards his own very private residence. They would pass by, he thought. They must pass by. But they were a long way from the U.N. camp, and Yoruba wondered why.

He stood by the window, looking out, watching the moiling mob stream down the street, seeing the jostling, hate-filled faces lunge nearer, watching them with the light of the dying sun blood-red in his eyes. He studied the members of this

mob closely. After all, they were —
indirectly — doing his work.

Isolated shots echoed through the
raucous chant of their voices. Expressions
were hard and vicious. Hands flailed the
air . . .

'Death! Death to the traitor!'

'Death! Death to the Baluba assassin!'

In that moment Yoruba's heart froze.

Then cold sweat bedewed his brow. He
mopped it away. *Baluba!* It couldn't
be . . . no one knew his secret . . . he was
imagining things.

But he wasn't imagining the men
who suddenly swarmed over his garden
wall. A half-brick struck the window
where he was standing, showering him
with sharp, cutting glass. He jerked
back quickly, blood streaming from a
cut over his eye. Fear welled up inside
him.

Then the front door crashed inwards.
Feet scrambled along the corridor. Men
poured into the room.

They ignored the body on the carpet.
Their gaze, furious and impassioned, was
riveted on him — Doctor Julius Yoruba.

'Traitor . . . Baluba dog . . . Lumumbist!'

Strong brown arms lunged at him. Hands wielded knives and chains and jagged bottles. He staggered under a rain of blows. From outside came the screaming voices of women: 'Bring him out! Give him to us! Bring him out!'

Yoruba tried to protest. 'A mistake! It's all a mistake!'

Words babbled hysterically from his lips. 'There — ' he tried to point at the body on the floor ' — there lies the traitor. I killed him with my hands! I — '

His speech was cut off by a savage blow.

He spat out blood, a gold tooth, tasted salt on his lips. Another blow smashed him down to his knees. The staring dead eyes of Stephan Trois seemed to mock him as he was dragged, screaming, from the room.

'No — no! You can't — '

He was thrust down the steps to face the howling mob. He tripped and sprawled and boots savaged him. A broken bottle jabbed home. A cycle chain slashed down. Arms pulled him this way and that. He went on protesting, blood sheeting his face, his babbling voice lost in the uproar.

'Kill him . . . kill him!'

He had no chance. No chance at all. And that was when, in the last moments of life, he realised that Stephan Trois had done this thing to him. Trois had told them that he was a Baluba; told them that he was the man behind the attempt on Tshombe's life. Trois had come to him in person to throw him to the mob.

Now the women had him. *Aaaargh — !* A scream ripped out of him. They gripped him by the arms, by the legs. And some went to work on his body while others pulled him this way and that . . .

He saw, in those horror-filled last moments of agony, Simon Brand trying to fight his way through the crowd to him, and he mumbled piteously, between screams, 'Brand — save me! Oh, save me!'

But Simon Brand had arrived too late. It had taken time to break Sam Wesley down. The mob had arrived before him.

The women had their hands on Julius Yoruba, and nothing and no one could save him now. Realising this, Brand slackened his efforts to reach him. He could do no good. No good at all. The intensity of the expressions of the people all around him showed him that. They would never listen to him. They were determined to exact a bloody revenge for the attempt on their leader's life.

Brand's work was done for him . . .

The women jerked and tugged at the limp body. They pulled Yoruba about like a rag doll. A bone snapped. A tendon tore. Yoruba's screams faded to blubbering sounds that were lost in the roar that rose to a ghastly crescendo above the streets of Elizabethville.

A wet bundle of bloody flesh — an arm — came flying through the air to land at Brand's feet.

There came a final roar of triumph from the crowd — and then silence. It was all over. Their blood lust sated, they melted way, and there in the wide avenue were a few limp pieces of flesh and bone; all that was left of Doctor Julius Yoruba.

He had paid dearly for his crimes.

Sickened, Brand surveyed the road that now had every appearance of a butcher's shop, and turned away.

17

Homeward Bound

'I'm well satisfied,' Cornelius Van Cleve said. 'You've done a good job, Mr. Brand. Both you, and Mr. Chandler. My principals and I — we are all deeply grateful.'

Deferentially, he handed Brand a crisp slip of paper. A cheque for a sum considerably in excess of the agreed ten thousand pounds. 'I trust that is in order. Mr. Brand — ?' he inquired somewhat anxiously of the detective, 'We undertook to meet your out-of-pocket expenses . . . I trust we have done so . . . ?'

'Very handsomely,' Brand agreed. And Cornelius Van Cleve leaned back in his chair. 'Good . . . good,' he said. 'And now that the formal purpose of this meeting is concluded, Mr. Brand, there are one or two points I'd be grateful if you'd clarify for me. One or two things I don't quite understand . . . '

He hesitated questioningly, settling his dark glasses more firmly on to the bridge of his beak of a nose. Simon Brand nodded.

They were gathered in the lounge of the Hotel Livingstone; Brand and Nick, Wallace and Angela De Villiers, and Cornelius Van Cleve. Overhead, a fan stirred the humid air as Brand finished his drink and lit a cigarette preparatory to answering all of the big Belgian's questions. Wallace prepared to listen avidly.

The *Morning Post's* Special Correspondent in Katanga appeared to have forgotten that his arm was round the blonde Angela's waist: fingering her silver belt with its pattern of nymphs and satyrs. Van Cleve had agreed they both deserved the inside story . . .

Brand said: 'Everything that happened stemmed from the character of Doctor Yoruba. He was a Communist sympathiser. Exactly how he wormed his way into President Tshombe's confidence we shall never know. But, somehow, he managed it. He was a fanatic, of course, absolutely dedicated to his cause. He was against an independent Katanga. He wanted Katanga a part of a Communist Congo, and he was working hand-in-glove with the men in power in Stanleyville in seeking to achieve this end.'

Brand paused thoughtfully for a moment, then he went on: 'Yoruba planned to have President Tshombe assassinated, take over control of the country himself, and join forces with the Communist politicians in the north. But he was on his own here in Elizabethville and he needed help to carry his plans through to success. So he took Trois as a partner. The cosmopolitan adventurer, Trois, wasn't interested in Congo power politics, only in what he could get out of the situation — and that made him useful to Yoruba.

'They were a fine pair: one dedicated and the other greedy, one seeking power and the other money . . . '

Simon Brand flicked ash into a glass tray, and drew again on his cigarette. 'It was Trois who handled the details. He hired Wesley, a professional killer, for the job of assassinating President Tshombe, and brought him up from Johannesburg in the guise of a mercenary. He employed M'Polo and his gang to take care of any loose ends — such as the Luvale boy, Nsambo, and Nsambo's mother. And he bought O'Donovan, who also wanted to feather his own private nest . . .

'The whole operation was well-planned and beautifully timed. It might well have succeeded. Tshombe's death was to be the signal for Gizengist forces to march south from Stanleyville — '

Van Cleve interposed quickly: 'That danger's already been averted, Mr. Brand. The President moved fast once he realised what was happening. Those troops won't get far!'

Brand inclined his head, and continued with his train of thought: 'At the same time, O'Donovan was to send in a false report on the situation to U.N. Headquarters in Leopoldville. A report designed to scare the U.N. authorities into panic action. With it, he enclosed a fully-detailed plan for a full-scale invasion of Katanga by United Nations' forces — a plan which, if acted upon, would have obscured from the eyes of the world what was really happening here until it was much, much too late. U.N. troops would have been used as a cover for the plotters' own bid for power. That letter was sent — '

'My God!' Van Cleve exploded. 'But why didn't you tell me this before, Brand? Something must be done — '

'Something was done,' Brand said gently. 'I did it. I extracted the false documents. I substituted blank sheets of paper. Right now, the United Nations Command in Leopoldville must be puzzling over those blank sheets. However . . . '

He blew a plume of cigarette smoke.

'About this time,' he said, 'Yoruba and Trois were beginning to come unstuck in more ways than one. Neither man really cared for, or trusted the other, that was the trouble. And when our two journalistic friends here turned up at Yoruba's house and chanced upon Trois there, Trois felt himself endangered. He gave our two friends credit for more perspicacity than they actually possessed, and I don't say that disparagingly, it's simply what happened. He thought that their curiosity might have been dangerously roused by the sight of his presence at Yoruba's house, and that they might somehow ferret out the facts of the criminal liaison between himself and the doctor. Consequently, he determined to get rid of our two friends. A major blunder on his part, as it turned out.'

'Just the same,' Wallace put in, 'if it hadn't been for you, Brand, it would have been curtains for us!'

And he spoke feelingly.

'Maybe so,' Brand agreed. 'But just look at what, in fact, happened. 'Wesley had to kill M'Polo to stop me getting him. And both of these men served the same master — Trois. They were both on the same side! This was dog-eat-dog with a vengeance!

'Simultaneously, by the very act of killing M'Polo, Wesley laid himself wide open to my deepest suspicions, and he also drew Angela's keen-eyed attention upon himself. This was really the beginning of the end, as we now know.

'Furthermore, as a result of all that

happened that day, the finger of dire suspicion pointed at Trois himself!

'For, it was immediately obvious to me as soon as I saw the body of the real chauffeur in the morgue, that M'Polo's impersonation of the man must have been planned at least a dozen hours in advance. And who knew of the car trip twelve hours in advance? Only Angela and Kirby, and Trois. So our cosmopolitan friend must have engineered all that transpired.'

Cornelius Van Cleve was frowning. 'I know it was so, but I don't quite follow you. You say that as soon as you saw the body of the real chauffeur in the morgue — '

'I knew that M'Polo's impersonation of the chauffeur could not have been the split-second, opportunist affair that Trois hoped it would seem,' Brand replied. 'The real chauffeur was murdered to give that idea credence, but it was patently fake. And this is why.

'M'Polo and the real chauffeur wore identical uniforms — except that one was about ten sizes larger than the other. Can't you see? M'Polo's uniform must have been made for him! It fitted him perfectly, and he was a much bigger man than the real chauffeur was. This indicated to me that some back-street tailor must have worked overtime on the job, and that the entire affair was planned minutely some hours in advance.

'And that, in turn, meant — as I've already explained — that Trois himself must have done the planning.'

'What a mind the man has!' Wallace marvelled. 'I'd suspected as much, of course. But suspicion is far from being proof. And, all the time, you'd worked it out with cast-iron certainty, Brand, and you knew — '

'I knew,' Brand agreed quietly. 'But — to press on —

'It was now O'Donovan's turn to die. So the death roll mounted. The girl, Crystal, was not so important. O'Donovan had simply set her the job of finding out what I was doing in Katanga.'

He gestured. 'And, in the end —

'In the end,' he said, 'Yoruba and Trois double-crossed each other. Yoruba poisoned Trois — who, unbeknown to the

252

Doctor, had in fact already betrayed him to the mob. And that's that!'

Briefly, and gratefully, he leaned back in his chair.

Then he said, 'For the time being, at least, the peace in this part of the world has been saved. And now all that remains is to catch a plane — '

'Not quite!' Cliff Wallace said. 'Whoa! Not so fast! First, let me get to a phone! I've got to file this story!'

And he beat Angela De Villiers to the phone booths by a short head.

Brand leaned back in his chair again — smiling. He lit another cigarette.

★　★　★

They were going home.

The silver bird of Sabena Airlines carried them high over Africa, flying north through brilliant sunshine to the grey gloom of England. Simon Brand and Nick Chandler were returning to Berkeley Square. They had finished their Congo assignment.

Cliff Wallace was travelling in the plane

with them. Jordan, editor of the *Morning Post*, had recalled him urgently. He was going back to his column 'Around and About' once more.

They left behind them an uneasy peace; but peace it was, and the people of the Congo and Katanga had a breathing space in which they might yet resolve their own problems successfully.

Brand and Nick Chandler had done their part. They had averted a murder that would have brought terrible bloodshed in its wake.

Now, perhaps, there would be a respite from the war and pestilence which had plagued that unhappy area of Africa for so long.

Brand looked forward to the day when the inheritors of the New Africa emerging from the cauldron of racial strife would learn to live their separate lives as good neighbours and true friends.

He hoped that day was close at hand.

THE END

We do hope that you have enjoyed reading this large print book.

Did you know that all of our titles are available for purchase?

We publish a wide range of high quality large print books including:
Romances, Mysteries, Classics General Fiction Non Fiction and Westerns

Special interest titles available in large print are:
The Little Oxford Dictionary Music Book, Song Book Hymn Book, Service Book

Also available from us courtesy of Oxford University Press:
Young Readers' Dictionary (large print edition) Young Readers' Thesaurus (large print edition)

For further information or a free brochure, please contact us at:
**Ulverscroft Large Print Books Ltd., The Green, Bradgate Road, Anstey, Leicester, LE7 7FU, England.
Tel:** (00 44) **0116 236 4325
Fax:** (00 44) **0116 234 0205**

Other titles in the
Linford Mystery Library:

MARKED FOR MURDER

Norman Lazenby

'Leave this affair alone, Martinson — Jean Hallison is dead . . . ' The caller had rung off, leaving Inspector Jim Martinson wondering if this was a bluff. Had Jean been murdered? And where did the suave, grinning Montoni fit in? He was accused of assaulting two women — but at the same time Jim himself had been watching him elsewhere. Now, however, Jim links the chain of evidence — slowly tightening the rope that will bring in the sinister gang that is terrorising Framcastle.

BURY THE HATCHET

John Russell Fearn

George Carter and his family lived peacefully in the small town of Uphill. But one fateful weekend something caused them to experience real fear and act completely out of character. The first trigger was when they learned that a homicidal maniac was at large in Uphill, carrying a damaged suitcase containing his victim's body parts. The second trigger was on finding that their new lodger's suitcase was also damaged — and the grisly truth of what was inside . . .

EXPERIMENT IN MURDER

John Russell Fearn

Moore dreams he's in the Lake District, climbing a mountain — carrying a woman's body — the woman he attacked as she slept in their hotel. He throws her body into the chasm at the summit and returns to the hotel. He wakes up. He examines his shoes: just as he left them before retiring, no trace of mud from the hillside . . . then it *has* all been a dream! But Moore, victim of an experiment in murder, finds his dream is real!